Why was her heart beating too fast?

Why did her mouth taste like copper? In the past few years she'd been in much more dire circumstances than being locked in Aunt Lillian's café with Truman.

"Are you happy in Garth?" Sadie asked.

"Most of the time." Truman's response was low and rumbling. A man's voice, not the voice of the boy she'd loved a very long time ago. No, not loved. Lusted after. Drooled over. That wasn't love. She just hadn't known it at the age of fifteen. He shifted his feet, crossed his arms over his chest. "You don't like it here."

"I don't know if I like it or not."

"So why are you so anxious to get out of town?"

Because I might start to feel like this is home again. Because I might fall in love with something here that I can't live without…. Maybe because I already have.

Dear Reader,

Love is in the air, but the days will certainly be sweeter if you snuggle up with this month's Silhouette Intimate Moments offerings (and a heart-shaped box of decadent chocolates) and let yourself go on the ride of your life! First up, veteran Carla Cassidy dazzles us with *Protecting the Princess*, part of her new miniseries WILD WEST BODYGUARDS. Here, a rugged cowboy rescues a princess and whisks her off to his ranch. What a way to go…!

RITA® Award-winning author Catherine Mann sets our imaginations on fire when she throws together two unlikely lovers in *Explosive Alliance*, the latest book in her popular WINGMEN WARRIORS miniseries. In *Stolen Memory*, the fourth book in her TROUBLE IN EDEN miniseries, stellar storyteller Virginia Kantra tells the tale of a beautiful police officer who sets out to uncover the cause of a powerful man's amnesia. But this supersleuth never expects to fall in love! The second book in her LAST CHANCE HEROES miniseries, *Truly, Madly, Dangerously* by Linda Winstead Jones, plunges us into the lives of a feisty P.I. and protective deputy sheriff who find romance while solving a grisly murder.

Lorna Michaels will touch readers with *Stranger in Her Arms*, in which a caring heroine tends to a rain-battered stranger who shows up on her doorstep. And *Warrior Without a Cause* by Nancy Gideon features a special agent who takes charge when a stalking victim needs his help…and his love.

You won't want to miss this array of roller-coaster reads from Intimate Moments—the line that delivers a charge and a satisfying finish you're sure to savor.

Happy Valentine's Day!

Patience Smith
Associate Senior Editor

Please address questions and book requests to:
Silhouette Reader Service
U.S.: 3010 Walden Ave., P.O. Box 1325, Buffalo, NY 14269
Canadian: P.O. Box 609, Fort Erie, Ont. L2A 5X3

Truly, Madly, Dangerously

LINDA WINSTEAD JONES

Silhouette®

INTIMATE MOMENTS™

Published by Silhouette Books

America's Publisher of Contemporary Romance

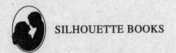 **SILHOUETTE BOOKS**

ISBN 0-373-27418-1

TRULY, MADLY, DANGEROUSLY

Copyright © 2005 by Linda Winstead Jones

LINDA WINSTEAD JONES

would rather write than do anything else. Since she cannot cook, gave up ironing many years ago and finds cleaning the house a complete waste of time, she has plenty of time to devote to her obsession for writing. Occasionally she's tried to expand her horizons by taking classes. In the past she's taken instruction on yoga, French (a dismal failure), Chinese cooking, cake decorating (food-related classes are always a good choice, even for someone who can't cook), belly-dancing (trust me, this was a long time ago) and, of course, creative writing.

She lives in Huntsville, Alabama, with her husband of more years than she's willing to admit and the youngest of their three sons.

She can be reached via www.eHarlequin.com or her own Web site www.lindawinsteadjones.com.

For my grandmother, Imogene Means,
who served up more than her share of Gelatin Surprise
in her ninety-nine years.

Prologue

"Behind you!"

Sadie dipped and turned, rolling across the creaking porch as a bullet smacked into the wall of the rustic cabin with a splintering crack. Still on her back, she lifted her pistol and took aim, but Santana leapt across the railing, grabbed the kidnapper's gun arm, and twisted it up and back until the weapon fell to the porch.

The first kidnapper they'd faced was already down—permanently—and Santana was handling the other just fine. Sadie scrambled up and carefully opened the front door of the isolated cabin on this Tennessee mountainside. The door squeaked loudly as it opened, and she stepped to the side so she wouldn't be a clear target for anyone waiting inside. The intelligence they'd collected told them there were only two kidnappers holed up in the cabin, but if she'd learned anything working for

Benning it was that you could never take anything for granted.

The main room was empty; the entire cabin was eerily silent. Her heart crawled into her throat. "Danny?" she said softly.

The young boy had been kidnapped five days ago, and his father had hired the Benning Agency to find him. The client was prepared to pay the ransom, if that was what it took. All he cared about was getting his son back safe and sound. All Sadie wanted was to be able to take the kid home, alive and healthy.

She glanced into the kitchen. Late-morning light spilled through an uncovered window. Beyond that window all she could see was sky and evergreen trees and the gold and red leaves of a Tennessee October. The view was beautiful, but the room was a mess.

She walked down the hallway without making a sound. The first bedroom she passed was as messy as the kitchen. And as deserted. The bathroom further down the hallway was small and unoccupied. That left one other room at the back of the hallway. The door was closed and locked from the hallway side.

Sadie holstered her pistol as Santana entered the hallway. She unlocked the door and opened it slowly.

Danny sat in the center of a big bed, bound and gagged and wearing the jeans and T-shirt he'd been wearing when he'd been snatched from the sidewalk in front of his home. Tears filled his eyes and stained his cheeks. He was apparently unhurt…but terrified.

Sadie smiled as she walked to the bed, allowing her jacket to fall over her weapon. She had a feeling Danny had seen enough guns for one lifetime.

"Hi," she said softly as she sat beside him and reached out to remove his gag. Duct tape. She pushed her anger deep.

"My name's Sadie, and this is Lucky." She nodded toward the man in the doorway. Santana was a couple of inches over six feet tall, and with his wide shoulders, big hands and killer stare he could be intimidating. Danny would respond best to a woman, they both knew that. "Your Dad hired us to come get you."

When the gag was removed, Danny took a deep, ragged breath. "My daddy sent you?"

Sadie nodded. How much had the kid heard of the struggle that had just taken place outside this cabin? It had become clear within minutes that the kidnappers were not willing to make a clean exchange. They were going to take the money, kill the kid and kill the lackeys who'd delivered the ransom. They hadn't counted on the lackeys being Sadie Harlow and Lucky Santana. Their bad luck.

At the very least, Danny must've heard the gunshots. "We scared away the men who kidnapped you," Sadie said calmly, "and now we're going to take you home."

Danny nodded enthusiastically.

Sadie reached into the pocket of her jeans. "I'm going to get a knife and cut the tape away from your hands and legs, is that all right?" She didn't want to flash a blade without warning the boy; she didn't know what the kidnappers had used to scare him.

Danny nodded, and she flicked the knife open with her thumb.

Santana backed away while she sliced at the duct tape. "I'm going to double check and make sure those bad guys are—uh—really gone," he said, leaving so he could move the body and the bound kidnapper to a place where the kid wouldn't have to see them.

When the duct tape had been peeled away, Sadie slipped the knife into her pocket and examined Danny's wrists and ankles. They were red and a little raw, but she'd seen worse. "Your daddy has been so worried about you," she said softly.

"He has?" Danny's blue eyes were wide and still damp with tears.

"Of course he has. We're going to call him right now, okay?"

Danny nodded enthusiastically.

Sadie retrieved her cell phone from a back pocket and dialed. After only one ring, Mr. Graham answered with a frantic, "Hello?"

"Mr. Graham, I have someone here who wants to speak with you." She handed the phone to Danny and stood. The kid gripped the small phone with both hands.

"Daddy?"

She stepped away from the bed for a moment to give Danny and his father some semblance of privacy. When she reached the doorway, Santana joined her. "All clear?" she asked softly.

He nodded.

A chill ran down Sadie's spine and her arms prickled. Adrenaline crash. She was coming down as if she'd been on a powerful drug. She'd done her best to be calm and cool with the kid, but in truth her heart was still pumping too hard and her skin was flushed and overly warm. It was always that way when bullets started flying.

She was starving.

Sadie glanced up at Santana, who watched the kid on the bed with calm, contented eyes. He looked like he'd just stepped out of a dull but satisfying business meeting.

The man was gorgeous, dark and fit and downright pretty. She liked him a lot as a person, and they worked together well. And no matter how tempting she might occasionally find him, it was never a good idea to mix business with pleasure. Santana didn't do emotion where sex was concerned, but she did. It was Sadie's downfall, the chink in her armor, her Achilles' heel. It was the reason she had been single in every way for the past several years.

"I'm thinking of taking a few days off," he said. "What about you?"

"I wish," she said softly. "I got an urgent phone call from my Aunt Lillian yesterday."

Santana turned his brandy-colored eyes to her.

"It's nothing, really, just…" No way was she going to tell Santana or any of her other co-workers—all males as testosterone-laden as he—why she was going back to Garth, Alabama. "I have to go home for a few days and take care of a little family business."

He didn't pry, but he did ask if she needed any help. She declined the offer, horrified at the very idea of anyone at the agency seeing her in the element she was about to jump back into. The Benning Agency was more than a P.I. firm. They didn't take on seedy divorce cases or investigate insurance scams. Instead, they provided top-notch security, rescued lost or kidnapped children like Danny and took on dangerous jobs no one else wanted. Their agents were the best of the best.

Sadie smiled at Danny as she walked to the bed to take the cell phone.

"It's going to take us a couple of hours to get you home," Sadie said as she scooped Danny's shoes off the floor and sat beside him. "Are you hungry?"

He nodded.

"Me, too. I could really use a nice, big chocolate milkshake right about now. And maybe some cheese fries and a chili dog."

Santana lifted one curious brow. "What gives, Harlow? You only eat like that when you're really nervous."

Sadie took Danny's hand as he left the bed then sent a tight smile at Santana. "I told you. I'm going home."

And it was going to take a lot more than a junk-food binge to soothe her nerves.

Chapter 1

The old saying "You can't go home again" was wrong. Sadie had quickly discovered that going home was easy. Much too easy. The saying ought to be, "You *shouldn't* go home again. Ever."

"Sadie," the intrusive, whispering voice interrupted what was left of her dream.

Sadie opened one eye, barely. The bedside clock glowed green in the dimly lit bedroom. Four-fifty—in the morning! She'd gotten to sleep about one-thirty, after unpacking, listening to Aunt Lillian's list of troubles and cousin Jennifer's hours of unending complaints and trying to adjust her body to this hard, less-than-welcoming bed.

"Go 'way," she mumbled as she closed her eye.

"It's almost five. Rise and shine!"

Rise and shine were words that should definitely be

justifiable cause for homicide, especially at this hour. With a moan, Sadie rolled onto her back and glared up, that one eye drifting open again. Lillian Banks stood five foot one, weighed maybe a hundred and five pounds, and carried her fifty-seven years as if it were thirty-seven.

"I didn't get to sleep until after one," Sadie said. Surely that was explanation enough, she thought as she closed her eye.

"Sadie," Aunt Lillian whispered.

The dream was right *there*. And it had been a good one. Hadn't it?

"Sadie." A nudge accompanied this more urgent call. The hard bed felt almost soft, she was so tired....

"Sadie Mae."

Sadie sat up as quickly as was possible considering her condition, and both eyes flew open. The sound of her full name usually did that to her. She didn't know if it was early years of maternal training or the horror of the full name that made her sound like a hick wearing a pair of cut-off overalls and straw in her hair. Whatever the reason, Aunt Lillian knew the trick. "I'm up!"

Lillian smiled widely. "Mary Beth called in sick. You'll have to work her shift."

This was so unfair. "Can't Jennifer do it?"

A shake of a gray head was her answer. "No. Jennifer was out late, and besides...she's got all the housekeeping to do and the last time she filled in for Mary Beth she spilt coffee on one of my best customers."

Sadie's airhead cousin, Lillian's own daughter, had spilled that coffee on purpose, no doubt, to save her from such early-morning abductions. Maybe Jennifer wasn't such an airhead after all. "Five minutes," Sadie said, drifting back toward the mattress.

It wasn't fair. Jennifer had gotten the normal name *and* the ability to weasel her way out of anything she didn't want to do.

Lillian tossed a dress at Sadie, a hideous, bubble-gum pink, lace-trimmed waitress uniform that actually had her name stitched over the pocket. Just plain Sadie, thank God.

"You had this made for me?" Her heart sank. Obviously her aunt expected that these early-morning duties were going to become a regular thing. Sadie asked herself again how she had ended up here. "I didn't come back to Garth to…"

"If you're going to help out until I get things in order around here, you need a proper uniform," Lillian said. "And don't give me that look. Waitressing is a perfectly acceptable occupation for a young lady."

Aunt Lillian was too embarrassed to tell her friends what had truly become of her niece. They all thought Sadie had gone to the big city and become a receptionist, suitable work for a young lady looking for a husband.

Pushing thirty—hard—wasn't young, and Sadie didn't want a husband. Almost been there, almost done that.

Lillian grinned and winked. "Hurry up. You know how early the fishermen show up for breakfast."

Once Sadie was sitting on the edge of the hard mattress, relatively awake, Lillian rushed from the room with a parting suggestion that her niece get crackin'.

Sadie crawled off the bed certain that she'd been tricked. Lillian wasn't all that desperate for help. She had just needed a free waitress during the one month a year that Garth was literally jumpin'. Only three weeks to the Miranda Lake Big Bass Festival, which arrived every October complete with parade, craft fair and—of course—bass tournament.

Since Uncle Jimmy's death four years earlier, Lillian had managed the Yellow Rose Motel, and the café across the parking lot, with the help of Jennifer and a few longtime employees. But one of those longtime employees had broken his leg last week, and another had gone and gotten herself pregnant a few months back. Lillian swore she couldn't hire just anyone. It took time and patience to find just the right person for the job.

Patience. Something Sadie did not possess.

There were financial problems, as well as a waitress shortage. A loan had come due, and for some reason the loan officer at the bank was being particularly stubborn. Financial problems Sadie could handle, though Lillian had put her foot down where a personal loan was concerned. She just wanted Sadie to meet with Aidan Hearn and reason with him. If she didn't know better, she'd think her staunch aunt was afraid of the man.

She'd tried to get that chore out of the way yesterday afternoon, immediately after her arrival. But Hearn's airhead secretary had insisted that the loan officer could not possibly see her without an appointment. It would be Thursday before he could squeeze her in. Two more days!

Once the financial concerns were taken care of, would Lillian let her niece go? Or did she think this waitress job that called Sadie out of bed at an ungodly hour was—horrors—permanent? Why hire a stranger when Sadie Harlow was the biggest sucker this side of the Mississippi?

The atrocious pink uniform dropped over her head. It was two sizes too big, at least. And closer inspection showed that someone else's name had previously been in the spot where *Sadie* was now embroidered in red. Not only was she wearing the ugliest uniform imaginable, it was a hand-me-down.

She opened her bedside drawer and eyed the pistol there. The sight eased her. The well-oiled weapon had a soothing kind of beauty, caught in the light of the bedside lamp. For the past five years, Sadie hadn't gone many places without that weapon close at hand. You only had to get in a jam once to get itchy about having some sort of protection nearby. No wonder she found the small pistol beautiful.

But there was no good place to conceal the weapon in the bubble-gum-pink uniform and thigh holsters were so damn uncomfortable. Maybe she didn't need to have her pistol within reach, for a change. There was nowhere on the planet safer than Garth, Alabama. The small town was quiet. Peaceful. Dull. Which is why Sadie had been so anxious to leave her home town eleven years ago.

She left her pistol in the bedside drawer and settled for a pocket knife, which sat heavily in a deep, very pink pocket.

"I can't believe I'm doing this," Sadie muttered as she walked down the stairs, again with only one eye open. That slit between tired lids was just enough to see where she was going as she made her way down to the motel lobby where Conrad Hudson—who helped out a couple of days a week and much preferred working nights—manned the desk. He'd been there last night, when Sadie had finally gone to bed. He greeted her in an annoyingly energetic voice. She grunted a surly good morning and stepped into the parking lot.

The Banks family lived above the front office and lobby, and had for as long as Sadie could remember. Right now only Jennifer and Lillian lived there, but in the old days the apartment had been crowded. Aunt Lillian and Uncle Jimmy, cousins Jennifer and Johnny. And then Sadie had come along to make everyone uncomfortable and to crowd the conditions even more.

She'd hated coming here after her mother's death. Orphaned, grieving and different, she had realized right away that she did not fit in well. Little Jennifer and her big brother Johnny had been blond and happy, good students who had lots of friends, while Sadie had barged in with tangled dark hair, shell-shocked by her mother's sudden passing and filled with an anger she couldn't explain away.

It had been just Sadie and her mother for so long, since Peter Harlow had died when his only child was a baby. To be thrust into family life was an additional shock all its own. Aunt Lillian had done everything possible to make the new member of her family feel like this place was home. And it had been, for a while.

But Sadie had left Garth as soon as possible after high school graduation. Had she been running away? Sure she had, though she hadn't known it at the time. She had run from the family who had taken her in, certain that somewhere out there was a place for her. A place where she didn't always feel different. A place where she *fit*. She'd dedicated herself to college for a few years, though she'd never found an area of study that she could fully embrace. She had about decided she'd be a career student, always at loose ends.

Then Spencer Mayfield had come along, with his slick ways and his "friendship" and his smooth seduction.

She'd come so close to actually marrying Spencer. The wedding date had been a mere two months away when she'd discovered that she wasn't his only "friend." Just as well. She really didn't want to go through life as Sadie Mae Mayfield.

The only men she trusted these days were her co-workers—Santana, Mangino, Cal, Murphy...even the Major. It had taken her a long time, but she'd finally found a place where she felt as if she truly fit in. And she didn't need anything else. The fact that she was the only female in a group of difficult men didn't faze her.

Sadie walked across the parking lot, yawning as she went, her white tennis shoes shuffling on the asphalt. Even though her coming here years ago had been sudden and tragic, in an unexpected way Garth still felt like home. Lillian and Jennifer were family. She had put down a few delicate and deep roots in her time here, but that didn't mean she wanted those roots to grow stronger and tie her to the place.

This afternoon she'd visit the bank *without* an appointment and have a word with Hearn about extending the loan. After that, she'd hire at least two new employees and see them settled in. And then, if she was very lucky, someone else would get themselves kidnapped and she'd be called away on urgent business.

Three days, tops, and she'd be outta here.

Why were so many people actually awake at five in

the morning? Dressed and disgustingly cheerful, the
patrons of Lillian's Café smiled and talked and…ugh,
was that guy flirting with her? Did he have something
in his eye or was he winking at her? She was in no
mood. Maybe that was the customer Jennifer had spilled
coffee on. Sadie hoped so.

She moved from booth to booth to table, pouring
coffee without spilling a drop. She scribbled breakfast
orders on a notepad and quickly squelched any unwanted overtures. The place was packed. Aunt Lillian
worked behind the counter, and Bowie Keegan, a thin,
short-haired young man who was the latest in a long line
of short-order cooks, worked the grill. Sadie was the one
who ended up scurrying from one end of the room to
the other, trying to take care of all the tables while Lillian handled the counter and some of the cooking. Sadie
did the best she could. If someone didn't get exactly
what they ordered, well, they *did* get fed. At this ungodly hour, they should be grateful.

"Sadie?"

She glanced down at the customer in the booth, a man
in a sharp khaki uniform, a deputy who grinned widely
at her. That smile was familiar, in an odd way. Wicked
and cocky and…Truman McCain. Please, not now.

"No," she said as she poured Truman a cup of coffee. "No Sadie here." She wore no makeup, was draped
in a hideous pink waitress uniform that was two sizes
too large, and she had a terrible case of bed-head. This
was no way to run into the guy she'd had a crush on during her impressionable fifteenth and sixteenth years.
Not that Truman, who had been her cousin Johnny's best
friend since they were five, had ever given Sadie the

time of day. "You must have me confused with someone else."

He pointed at her breast. "It says Sadie right there."

"Borrowed uniform."

"You look vaguely familiar," he teased.

"I get that from a lot of people. Are you ready to order?"

Truman just smiled. Why did he have to look so good? A good three years past thirty he still had all his hair, which was a lovely warm brown that curled a little at the ends, just as she remembered. His eyes remained undulled by time. They were a fabulous shade of blue—not too dark, not too light—that seemed to see right through her. He was bigger, wider in the shoulders and maybe a little taller, though it was hard to tell with him sitting in the booth that way. He just seemed… larger than she remembered.

The man who had provided her with the most humiliating moment of her life should not have aged so well. It just wasn't fair.

"Do you need a few more minutes to decide?" she asked.

He ordered the special and she walked away, too aware that his eyes were on her legs that needed shaving, her too-big uniform, and her tangled hair. Her ill-advised return home was not getting any better.

Truman's smile faded as he watched Sadie walk away. He hadn't thought much about Sadie Harlow, at least not recently. She must've had a rough time of it. Poor thing, she didn't look so good. She was pale and there were circles under her eyes. And she must've lost weight. That dress hung on her.

The legs beneath that dress were not so bad, though, he mused as his gaze landed there.

He knew damn well she hadn't forgotten him, even if it had been more than eleven years since he'd seen her. If nothing else, the sheer terror in her eyes when she'd recognized him had given her away.

She delivered his breakfast without looking him in the eye, letting the heavy white plate laden with eggs and grits and biscuits land on the table too hard. His check followed, slapped onto the table near the edge. He mumbled a polite thanks and let her walk away. Whatever happened to forgive and forget?

Truman took his time with his breakfast, watching the sun come up. It would be another slow day, he imagined. Most of his days as a deputy for this small Alabama county were. There was crime here, there just wasn't much of it. And it was minor stuff, usually. Some days he felt more like an errand boy than a deputy. He changed tires, picked up prescriptions for a couple of the old folks who didn't—or shouldn't—drive, and kept kids out of trouble. He broke up the occasional fight, and had driven home more than his share of drunks. It wasn't the life he'd planned for himself, but he liked it. Most days.

Breakfast finished, he slid out of the booth, taking care with his right leg as he always did. His limp had improved so it was barely noticeable. Or maybe he was just getting used to it. He dropped a bill on the table.

As he approached the counter, his check and a five-dollar bill in hand, Lillian gave him a wide smile. "'Morning, Deputy Truman," she said brightly. "Was everything all right?"

"Wonderful as usual," he said as he handed over his

check, waiting as she opened the register and counted out his change. Behind Lillian, Sadie wiped furiously at the counter and kept her head down—and her back to him. On purpose? Surely not. While Lillian placed his change in the palm of his hand Sadie escaped, taking the long way around the counter and wiping down recently vacated tables. She put an awful lot of energy into cleaning those tables, Truman noticed as he headed for the door.

"Have a nice day, Miz Lillian." Truman pushed against the glass door and glanced over his shoulder. "You, too, Sadie Mae," he said, casting a grin at her back.

He was still grinning when she flew out the door, not ten seconds behind him. "What is this?" she asked.

He turned around to find Sadie waving a five-dollar bill in his face. She didn't look so tired and worn-out anymore. There was color in her cheeks, fire in her eyes, and instead of being simply tangled, her dark hair looked sexy and wild. He liked it. It struck him at that moment that Sadie Harlow had grown up quite nicely.

"Your tip?"

"Your entire breakfast didn't cost five dollars," she said, still thrusting the bill in his direction. "And I didn't even refill your coffee!"

"Yeah, I noticed that."

"Take it back," she ordered.

"No." Truman leaned against the fender of his patrol car.

Sadie took a single step toward him. "I'm warning you, McCain."

"Are you threatening an officer of the law?" he teased.

"Just take it!" She took another step forward. "And don't you ever, *ever,* call me Sadie Mae."

"Let's make a deal," he said. "I call you whatever you want me to, and you keep the tip."

"I don't want you to call me anything," she said, her voice softer as she came closer. "And I certainly don't want your…your pity tip!"

He couldn't help himself. He laughed. "Pity tip?"

"Well, what else would you call it? I gave you lousy service."

On purpose, he was sure. "Yeah, but I figure you have potential. One day you're going to be a great waitress."

"Bite me," she said, stepping forward to slip the five-dollar bill into his breast pocket.

"When did you get back?" he asked before she could make a quick escape.

"Yesterday."

"How long are you going to stay?"

He saw the *not very long* in her dark eyes, but she answered, "A few days. The family just, you know, needed some help."

"Johnny couldn't make it?"

Sadie rolled her eyes. "My hot-shot cousin is much too busy to be bothered. Since I was available…" She shrugged. "Here I am."

Sadie was surly, she was not happy to be here…and still there was something about her that made Truman want to smile. "Working lunch today?"

"Not if I can help it. Sorry if I was rude," she added, turning around slowly to return to the coffee shop.

Truman took the five from his pocket and rolled it up tight between his fingers. "Sadie?"

She obediently turned around, and he stepped forward to drop the bill down the front of her too-big uniform. If his aim was even halfway decent, it would get caught in her bra. "Have a nice day."

Sadie sputtered and went in after the five, but by the time she had it in her hand Truman was behind the wheel and backing out of the parking lot.

Things could not possibly get any worse. All she wanted was a nap. Half an hour. Maybe forty-five minutes. Jennifer leaned over the bed. "I am not cleaning up that mess," she whined.

Sadie didn't bother to argue with her cousin. Arguing with Jennifer was always a waste of breath. No matter how logical the argument, Jen refused to lose. "I thought this was your regular job," Sadie said as she left the bed.

"Yeah, but I have to draw the line somewhere," Jennifer whined. "Room 119 is a *mess*."

"You already said that," Sadie grumbled.

"And it *stinks*."

Jennifer was an apparent afterthought, eight years younger than Sadie, a full eleven years younger than her brother, Johnny. Lillian had always claimed that she'd been too old when she'd had Jennifer. She hadn't had the energy to handle a difficult child. From the outside it had always looked to Sadie as if it had become easier for Lillian and Jimmy to let Jennifer have her way than to discipline the brat.

At the moment, Sadie couldn't even remember what it was like to be twenty-two. And she had never been spoiled the way Jennifer had.

Johnny was the only Banks son, the eldest, the responsible one. He was a real-estate bigwig in Dallas, and made it to Garth only slightly more often than Sadie did. Jennifer was the baby, pretty and pampered, coddled by the entire family. Why should she leave? She had it made here. Sadie was still the oddball, caught in the middle and never quite feeling like she was part of the family, even though they had all done their best to make her feel like one of them.

"You'll do it?" Jennifer practically wailed.

"Yes, I'll do it," Sadie said. At least she had traded in her pink waitress uniform for something more palatable—jeans and a plain white T-shirt. Of course, over this she added an apron with several pockets, deep pockets that held cleansers, plastic bags and rags for wiping down counters and desktops. Not exactly her dream outfit.

"You'll help, right?" she asked, just as Jennifer turned in the opposite direction.

"No way," Jen yelled. "That room *stinks*."

"Great. It *stinks*." Sadie glanced across the parking lot to the busy Lillian's Café. A county patrol car was parked near the door. Truman's? Surely not. There were other places in Garth to eat lunch. Not many, but a few.

If she hadn't known better, she would have thought he'd been flirting with her this morning. Ha. Even if he had been, it was a waste of time. He'd had his chance, and he'd blown it. She took some small measure of comfort in knowing that she *could* kick his ass, if she wanted to.

Not quite fourteen years ago she'd offered her virginity to Truman, and he'd turned her down. In retrospect, she'd been a kid and he probably hadn't wanted to go to jail, but still…he shouldn't have laughed. The rejection had been humiliating enough, but for him to laugh at her when she'd been so in love and decidedly serious about seducing him, that was just wrong.

She wasn't sixteen any more, and she wasn't a lost little girl clinging to what she thought was love. But the truth of the matter was, she still found Truman just a little bit too attractive. Her childish infatuation had died a long time ago, but she still had a soft spot for the guy. The last thing she needed was to get involved with a man from Garth. She'd never escape. She'd be effectively and completely sucked in. Instead of quick trips where she stayed a couple of hours, tops, she'd be forced to remain here for days at a time.

Like now.

Best to avoid Truman as much as possible, Sadie decided stoically. Aunt Lillian would just have to find someone else to take the morning shift if Mary Beth called in sick again. Sadie was desperate. If she had to spill coffee on some poor unsuspecting customer to get out of waitress duty, so be it.

Even better, she'd hire a new waitress ASAP.

The cart laden with towels, toilet paper and cleaning supplies was still parked outside room 119. Sadie knocked, shouted, and then used her key to open the door. The room was, as Jennifer had said, a mess. The covers on the bed had been torn off, drawers were opened and one was even on the floor. A bottle of wine had been emptied…all over the floor and the bed. Crackers had been crushed and scattered, too, and so had what looked to be cubes of cheese.

And Jen hadn't been kidding when she said it smelled. Oh, what *was* that? The cheese? Sadie leaned over the bed and sniffed at a cube. Yikes, that was part of it.

She snapped on a pair of latex gloves. Trash can in one hand, she walked around the room picking up offensive garbage. Food, mostly, along with the occasional wrapper or empty bottle. She couldn't believe that there were people out there who didn't pick up after themselves in the most basic way. What slobs.

A bottle of spray cleaner and a soft rag worked wonders on the nasty surfaces. Still, there was only so much a good scrubbing could do. She stripped off the sheets, being very careful that only the latex gloves came into contact with the linens. Yikes. No matter how bad her life got from here on out, she could always be assured that there were women out there who had it worse.

Linens stripped, Sadie snagged her trash can once again. As she neared the bathroom, the smell that had hit her as she'd walked into the room got worse. Holding her breath, she leaned over a small trash can just outside the bathroom, expecting to find a stack of nasty diapers. Nothing.

A knock on the open door made Sadie jump and turn. She squinted. A shadow filled the doorway, cutting off the sunlight. A tall, broad-shouldered shadow.

Truman leaned against the door jamb and grinned. "A woman of many talents," he teased.

Sadie walked toward the door. She was in no mood… "What are you doing here?"

Truman stepped back as she exited 119. Fresh air had never smelled so sweet.

"I thought I saw you head into this room," Truman said.

"Please tell me you're not stalking me," she responded casually, not looking him in the eye.

"Of course not. That would be illegal."

She'd had enough. "Truman McCain, what the hell do you want?"

Most men would take the hint and retreat. Sadie had gotten very good at telling a man to back off with nothing more than a *look*. Most of them didn't just back off, they slunk away with their gaze pinned to their shoes. But not Truman. He held his ground. His smile didn't go away. Not completely. "Dinner," he finally said.

A date. He was actually asking her out on a *date*. "You've got to be kidding."

"Nope. I never kid about such serious matters."

Sadie didn't beat around the bush, not anymore. She didn't give lame excuses, she didn't worry about hurting any man's feelings. Did they have feelings? She thought not.

"You want to feed me?" she said sharply. "Fine. But I am not sleeping with you. Not now, not ever. So if this is your slick country-boy way of trying to worm your way into my bed, forget it. You had your shot, and you blew it." She crossed her arms over her chest.

Truman didn't seem at all offended or dismayed. "I thought we could have dinner and catch up. That's all." He leaned slightly toward her. "I don't want to sleep with you, either, Sadie. You're a lousy waitress, and you smell like something nasty I stepped in down by Ted Felton's farm last week." His smile never wavered. "Literally. Seven o'clock? I'll pick you up."

Oh, she was going to regret this. Quickly, she reasoned that if she was out for a few hours, she couldn't watch the desk, field phone calls, or dish up grits and coffee. Besides, deep inside she was not entirely opposed to dinner with Truman.

"Seven-thirty," she said.

Business done, she turned and walked away from Truman McCain. No, that was not a little bubble of excitement in her chest. There was nothing to get excited about. They'd eat, she'd ask questions about what had happened to him in the past eleven years—like she didn't already know—and if Truman did dare to make a move she'd put him in his place so fast he wouldn't know what hit him.

Sadie was actually smiling when she opened the bathroom door, but the smile didn't last. The stench hit her so hard she reeled back a split second before she realized what she was seeing in the bathtub.

She backed away from the half-open door, her eyes on the body in the tub. A part of her mind logically catalogued the details. Male. Naked. Definitely dead, probably for hours. She didn't recognize him, but then… would she, even if she knew who the man had once been? The face was distorted, and the neck…what was left of it…was…oh…

Another part of her mind screamed silently. *Run.*

After a few seconds, Sadie listened to that command. She turned and ran to the door. Truman wasn't even halfway across the parking lot.

"McCain!" she shouted.

He stopped and turned, a half grin on his face. "You didn't change your mind already, did you?" His smile faded, and he walked toward her with that slight limp that still surprised her, even though she knew what had happened. "What's wrong?"

Sadie moved back, clearing the doorway so Truman could step into the room. "You need to call somebody," she said softly. "There's a dead man in the bathtub."

His eyes snapped in that direction, and he moved past her. "Stay here," he ordered in a soft voice.

As if she had to be told. She'd seen enough, thank you very much.

A glance was all Truman needed. He backed away, took Sadie's arm, and led her outside. Grabbing the two-way radio that hung from his belt, he alerted dispatch of the situation. That done, he looked down at her without a smile, without even a speck of that McCain charm.

"Did you disturb anything?"

"Hell, Truman, I cleaned the room. All but the bathroom. I disturbed just about everything."

He muttered the word that was very much on Sadie's mind, a word that would have shocked Aunt Lillian out of her orthopedic shoes.

"I didn't vacuum," Sadie said. "And all the garbage I collected is in one bag."

"Good."

"Did you recognize him?" Sadie asked, curiosity pushing aside her early revulsion.

"No, but then I didn't take a really close look."

"I understand completely," Sadie said honestly. Already she heard approaching sirens.

People didn't get murdered in Garth, and from what little she'd seen she was pretty sure the man in room 119's bathtub had not committed suicide. He'd been murdered, in a very ugly way.

Truman leaned slightly forward as the first patrol car

pulled wildly into the parking lot. "I've always wanted
to do this," he whispered.

"What?" she snapped.

"Sadie Mae Harlow, don't leave town."

Chapter 2

After stripping out of the outfit she'd been wearing when she'd found the body and then showering vigorously, Sadie had gladly changed into clothing she was more comfortable in. A pair of black pants that had a little stretch in them, sturdy boots, a leather jacket and a shoulder holster, where her pistol now rested. After what she'd seen today, she needed her weapon close.

She was still tempted to head down to the bank and insist on seeing Hearn. Two days was a ridiculous amount of time to wait to see a loan officer at a small town bank. There had been a framed photo of the man hanging in the outer office, where Sadie had done battle with the receptionist. Hearn was sixtyish, with a full head of gray hair and pale-blue eyes. Not bad looking for an older man, but he had that cocky smile that men who consider themselves better than everyone else can't seem to wipe from their faces, no matter how hard they try. He was a VP, or some such, which didn't mean much in such a small bank. He couldn't possibly be booked until Thursday afternoon.

Besides, she needed something to take her mind off finding the body. She'd seen a lot of bad stuff, working for the PI agency in Birmingham and then for Benning, but she'd never run across a body that had been stewing for hours. She would never forget that smell, or the complete and utter deadness of the man in the tub. There had been no life left, not even a hint that he had been a living breathing man not so long ago. She shuddered and pushed the feeling aside. She couldn't afford weakness of any kind, not in her profession.

She still had no idea who the man in Room 119 might be. Conrad Hudson, who had checked the man in late last night, had already left for the day when the body was discovered. The sheriff had sent a deputy—not Truman, but some horribly young and enthusiastic boy—to Conrad's house to speak with him, but no one was home. Since Conrad spent every spare moment fishing, he was probably on the lake somewhere. He'd be found. Eventually.

The name in the register was a suspicious 'Joe Smith,' and the man had paid for the room in cash.

Drugs, probably, Sadie reasoned. A drug deal had gone bad and Smith, or whoever he was, had been murdered because of it. She would have to have a talk with Lillian about renting her rooms to just anyone who came along. Lillian was so naive, she probably never considered that anything illegal might go on at her motel. It was a family place, a simple motel that had seen good years and lean. Once a bad element moved in, it would be tough to save the Yellow Rose Motel.

Truman had taken a brief statement from Sadie at the scene and he'd taken control of the evidence, basically keeping everyone out until the proper team arrived to catalog everything. The Alabama Bureau of Investigation would be called in, since neither the city of Garth nor the county had the resources to investigate a murder. Those investigators would want to question her soon, but while she waited she might as well see about getting the reason for her trip out of the way.

Maybe Hearn would agree to allow Sadie to repay her aunt's loan without letting Lillian know. It would take Sadie a few days to get her hands on that much cash, but it could be done.

"Sadie!" Jennifer ran up the stairs, shouting as she entered the living quarters.

Sadie stepped into the hallway. "What's wrong now?" There was always a crisis of some sort around here. As long as it wasn't another body...

"The ABI investigator, he wants to talk to you," Jennifer said breathlessly.

"He's here?"

Jen nodded. "And he does not look very happy."

Sadie headed for the stairs. "Murder isn't happy business."

"Yeah, but he looks really *pissed*."

"He probably got called in off the golf course." Sadie pushed into the lobby, to find that it was quite crowded. Truman stood back a ways, positioned near the door, and a red-eyed Aunt Lillian sat in a rickety chair near

the front desk. She'd been upset when Sadie had gone
upstairs to dress, but now she was obviously shaken.

The man standing between Sadie and Truman eyed
her suspiciously. "I was working a cold case, actually.
I don't golf."

Sadie saw no reason to respond.

"Investigator Wilson Evans." The stocky brown-
haired man didn't offer his hand.

"Sadie Harlow." Instinctively, she looked toward
Truman, who remained stony-faced as he fixed his gaze
on her.

"We've identified the victim," Evans said, his voice
even and cool.

"That's good."

In the moment of silence that followed Sadie's response, she automatically looked to Truman McCain.
For a reason she refused to explore, she was glad he'd
stayed.

"Aren't you curious?" Evans looked Sadie up and
down with suspicious eyes. She suspected he was
sharper than he looked.

Aunt Lillian's breath hitched and she made an odd
noise that caught in her throat, as if she stifled a cry.

"Not really," Sadie said honestly. "I don't know many
people in Garth anymore, and I seriously doubt…"

"Do you know Aidan Hearn?"

The mention of the banker's name startled Sadie so
much she blinked hard and leaned slightly back.
"Hearn? Not really. Was that…" She tried to envision
the possibility that the smiling man in the photo at the
bank and the grotesque thing she'd found might be one
and the same.

"I understand you made a bit of a scene in his office yesterday afternoon."

Sadie's eyes cut to Truman again. He didn't smile, he didn't offer silent comfort. At the moment he looked as cold as Evans. "I would hardly call it a scene," she answered.

The detective flipped open his notebook and read from the small page. "You called him a tyrant..."

"He wasn't there," Sadie explained.

Evans didn't so much as slow down. "And you intimated that if he didn't see you *immediately,* he'd be sorry."

"I had an appointment for Thursday."

"You called his secretary a bimbo..."

"She is," Sadie said beneath her breath.

"And on your way out of the room you kicked over a small trash can."

"It had been a long day and the trash can was empty. Mostly."

Evans flipped the notebook shut. "Do you have an uncontrollable temper, Miss Harlow?"

"Of course not!" she shouted.

Truman crossed his arms over his chest and shook his head, a little, and suddenly Sadie was eleven again, out of place and alone and feeling as if the world was conspiring against her.

"It's my fault," Lillian said softly.

All eyes turned her way. "What?" Sadie asked.

"I sent her there to speak to Mr. Hearn. He refused to even listen to my pleas, and I was afraid I'd lose the motel and the café if I didn't get an extension on the loan. I called Sadie because I couldn't think of another way." Lillian lifted her head and looked squarely at Evans. "Sadie might lose her temper, and she might kick over a garbage can or say something she doesn't mean on occasion. That mouth of hers has gotten her into trouble all her life."

"Aunt Lillian…" Sadie began. This kind of "help" wasn't going to help matters at all.

"But she would never hurt a living soul."

Lillian had no idea how many living souls her niece had hurt. But they had all been bad guys who deserved what they got, and Sadie had never killed anyone in cold blood. Actually, she'd never killed anyone, not even bad guys. But she had wounded more than her share…

It took only a few minutes for Evans to take Sadie's statement, while Lillian and Truman looked on. It was an oddly informal interview, allowable due to the unusual circumstances. From a certain vantage point in the office, Sadie could look through the window and see the investigators and deputies gathered around room 119. They used crime-scene tape to cordon off the area, and it wasn't long before an ambulance arrived. They wouldn't be allowed to move the body until Evans gave the okay, but they were ready. And curious.

Sadie moved to the counter where Conrad would've been standing last night. The door to 119 was clearly visible.

"Conrad must've seen whoever went into that room with Hearn," Sadie said. "There's a street lamp almost directly overhead."

"We've got deputies and ABI agents searching for him," Evans snapped.

Sadie's stomach roiled, a little. She had learned always to listen to that gut reaction. "I think maybe you'd better find him quick. I have a feeling that whoever murdered Hearn won't hesitate to take out anyone they think might be a witness."

She recognized the new surge of emotion as outrage. Maybe she couldn't wait to get out of Garth all over again. But by God, it just wasn't right for people to get murdered here.

Sadie in tight black pants, her hair combed and her cheeks flushed pink, painted an entirely different picture than the tired woman in the ill-fitting pink uniform who'd made such a poor waitress that very morning.

Truman really did want to believe that Lillian was right and Sadie didn't have it in her to murder anyone. But she did have a temper, and to be honest he didn't know her anymore. She'd left home a girl and come home a woman, and who knows what had happened to her during the years in-between?

When he'd told Sadie not to leave town, he'd been— at least in part—jesting. When Evans delivered the same order, he wasn't kidding at all. And Sadie knew it. A local man was dead, killed the same night she'd arrived in town for the specific purpose of seeing Hearn and convincing him to extend her aunt's loan.

Since she'd cleaned the room, she had a very plausible reason for any of her own fingerprints that were found on the door knob. Not that there would be many fingerprints lifted from any other surface. Sadie—who had been wearing gloves to clean—had scrubbed every surface in the motel room.

She hadn't touched the bathroom, though, and that

was a good sign. And the discovery of the body had obviously disturbed her. Either that, or she had turned into a great actress.

She had definitely turned into a beautiful woman. Sadie wasn't traditionally pretty, like her cousin. But she was the kind of woman who would always make heads turn, and he was certain that when she walked into a room men between the ages of fifteen and ninety muttered a drawn-out, appreciative *damn*.

His study of Sadie was interrupted by occasional bouts of hysteria from Lillian Banks. She'd lose it for a moment, then rein herself in and settle into silence. Was that fear in her eyes? Or plain old horror at knowing that a man had been killed in her motel and her niece was—for the moment at least—a suspect.

Logic aside, he didn't think Sadie was guilty. Not of murdering Hearn, at least. But one thing was clear.

Women like Sadie Harlow weren't content to stay in a place like Garth. She was here to help her family, but as soon as she was able she'd be gone.

"Be back by ten," Jennifer said as she plopped down on the end of Sadie's bed. "I'm supposed to work the front desk since Conrad still hasn't shown up, but I have plans. I figured since you're here you can do me a favor and fill in for me."

Sadie didn't argue that what she really needed was a good night's sleep, or that it was entirely possible Conrad would show up late. It wouldn't be the first time, from what she heard. "It's Tuesday," she said as she applied a bit of mascara. "What sort of plans could you possibly have?"

"Just…plans."

Sadie sighed. She'd probably be home by nine. Still, it galled her a little that her flighty cousin had such an active social life, while she had none. Thirty wasn't all that old. Why did she feel ancient?

No, she wouldn't be thirty for two more weeks. Would she officially become a spinster over a cake with too many candles? Sitting alone in her small apartment, with her girlie things around her and the television on and… What was she thinking? The day's excitement had addled her brain. Since a social life usually included men in some form or another, she was definitely better off without one. Bring on the spinsterhood.

Not that she wanted to look like a spinster…

It was strange, to be getting ready for her first date in ages when just this afternoon she'd stumbled across a dead body. Jen had commented on the tragedy and the *smell*, and then she'd shuddered and changed the subject. Unpleasant things did not deter Jennifer Banks. She ignored them completely so they barely slowed her down.

"I'll be home before ten," Sadie promised, wondering if she could even stay awake that long.

"Nice dress," Jennifer said, relieved and smiling once again. "It looks expensive."

"It is," Sadie said. The classic little black dress was her favorite. True, it made concealing her revolver a problem, but in this instance she'd deal with the discomfort of a thigh holster.

"If it was a couple sizes smaller, I might ask if I could borrow it."

Sadie sighed, but did not growl or even turn to glare at her skinny cousin.

"Can I borrow those earrings sometime?" Jennifer asked, leaning to the side to get a better look at the diamond studs.

"Not on your life."

In the mirror, Sadie watched as Jen stuck out her tongue. Some things never changed.

Sadie applied a little bit of hairspray to her curling dark hair, and then she dabbed some perfume behind her ears, just in case any of the day's excitement had left a lingering odor that hadn't scrubbed out in the shower. Eggs and grits, cheese, ammonia…and other things she'd rather not think of right now.

"You're going to give poor old Truman a heart attack."

"Why's that?" Sadie asked absently.

"You look great, that's why," Jennifer said. "Makeup, sexy dress, perfume. The whole works. Trust me, no one around here looks like this. Are you guys, you know…"

"No," Sadie said forcefully. "We're just friends. There is no 'you know.' I'm not getting dressed up for Truman," she added in a sensible voice. "I'm dressing for myself. I like to look nice now and then." She'd had enough of bubble-gum-pink uniforms and maid's aprons for one day.

"Yeah, right," Jennifer said, a wicked smile on her face and in her voice. When Sadie stepped into her black heels, Jennifer whistled. "You can't tell me you're wearing those monsters for yourself. They look great, but that heel is a killer. Those shoes," Jennifer said with a wag of her fingers, "say, *Take me Truman, take me now.* Why don't you just go naked and save yourself all this trouble? Ten o'clock, Sadie. I swear, if you're not home by ten, I'll…I'll…"

"Send the sheriff after us?"

"Not a bad idea."

Sadie walked across the room. Okay, so she hadn't worn these heels in ages. They were not comfortable, not at all. But they did look great, she knew that. Maybe she wasn't tiny like Jennifer, but she was tall, and she had long legs and decent breasts, and when she put some effort into it she could look good.

Not for Truman, she insisted silently, but for herself. Her first full day in Garth had been a kicker, and she needed to turn her mind in a new direction. Just for to-night. Tomorrow she'd be back to being desk clerk, maid and waitress. But not for long. Hearn must've been involved in something nasty to get killed the way he had. Evans would find the evidence and the murderer, and he'd send Sadie on her way with an insincere apology.

Sadie didn't belong here any more now that she had at the age of eleven.

Sadie was overdressed for Bob's Steak and Fixin's, but then she was probably overdressed for anything this side of Birmingham. Since Truman had worn jeans and a nice cotton button-up shirt, she was definitely over-dressed for him. She'd done this to get back at him, he imagined, to repay him for telling her not to leave town or for sticking her tip in her bra.

Truman tried not to let on that he was at all affected by the red lips, the black dress, the long legs or the way she walked in those heels. When had Sadie Har-low gotten so gorgeous? She'd always been cute, his best friend's little cousin who had a crush on him. Back in those days she'd had a tendency to show up wherever he and Johnny happened to be. He hadn't minded her tagging along now and then, not the way Johnny had. He'd always thought she was kinda sweet. But he'd been caught up in the high-school-jock thing and she'd seemed so young. Plus she'd never had this effect on him. And if she had, Johnny would have killed him.

It was a cruel form of punishment, he imagined. Sadie's way of waving a red flag in his face. Look what you could have had. Look what you'll never have. Look, but do not touch. He should have accepted his mother's invitation to go home for a nice, safe dinner of chicken and dumplings and left Sadie alone.

His motives had been honorable. She was exhausted and needed a couple of hours away from the motel. A friendly meal and conversation, that's all he'd had in mind when he'd suggested dinner. Really.

He hadn't known she'd stumble across a dead body minutes after grudgingly accepting his invitation. And he definitely hadn't expected *this*. He was on edge, wound so tight every muscle in his body had tensed. He looked at Sadie sitting there, all dolled up and grown up, and all he could think about was getting her naked. It had been a long time since he'd wanted any woman this way.

"Are you sure we should be doing this?" she asked. "Having dinner together doesn't seem at all ethical, given the circumstances."

"Why not? I'm not investigating the murder."

"We're just old friends sharing a meal, and the fact that we found a dead man a few hours ago means nothing," she said.

"Yeah."

She played with the food on her plate, and her eyes scanned the restaurant almost casually. Almost.

Truman gladly studied the full red lips, the curve of her cheek, the fire in her eyes. Yeah, naked would be good. "So, how long have you been a PI?"

Sadie didn't drop her fork, but her head snapped around. She glared at him, dark eyes flashing. He'd managed to surprise her. Good.

"You've been poking around in my life? You said you didn't have anything to do with investigating the murder."

"Actually, I did a quick search on you this morning, after breakfast and before you found that body."

Sadie pursed her lips and lifted her chin. She wasn't the same little girl who'd followed him and Johnny around. She'd gotten tough.

"Lillian likes to tell everyone that I'm a receptionist in Birmingham."

"I know. Where's the gun?" he asked.

She did her best to look innocent.

"I know you have a permit. This afternoon you were wearing it under your jacket, neatly concealed. Where is it now?"

She didn't bother to deny that she was carrying. "In a place where you'll never have the chance to find it."

He grinned. Yeah, he liked her tough. He liked her all grown-up. "So, how did you end up a PI? Seems like nasty work for a pretty girl."

Sadie smiled. "I'm not pretty, I'm not a girl, and the work is only occasionally nasty."

Truman wasn't looking for a fight, so he didn't bother to argue about the pretty thing. Surely Sadie knew how gorgeous she was. Pretty women, they always knew. "Okay. But that doesn't answer my question."

She relaxed a little, and leaned forward. "I fell into it. I was supposed to get married, but it didn't work out. I was tired of knocking around college without knowing what I wanted to do with my life, and I needed a way to pay the bills." She smiled. "I found a job working as a receptionist for a small PI agency. Strictly temporary, of course." Something in her smile changed, turned more genuine. "I'd been there three months when a displeased client came barging in with a gun in his hand. He used me as a shield, and I spent the better part of an afternoon wondering if I was about to die."

Nothing to smile about. "And you didn't quit then and there?"

Sadie shook her head. "You know me, Truman. I got mad, and I decided I was never going to be helpless again. My boss, Larry Myrick, saw that I got training. Basic self-defense first, then firearms, knife-work, karate. I liked it. I got good. And Larry offered me a job as an investigator."

"Why have I never heard any of this?"

"Because Aunt Lillian thinks my chosen career is scandalous." Her eyebrows danced. "Chasing bad guys is not at all ladylike."

"You're still working for Myrick?" He knew she wasn't, but he did wonder how she'd answer. The Benning Agency was miles away from a small PI office in Birmingham. Literally and figuratively.

She shook her head. "No. I was recruited by a larger agency a few years back."

That out of the way, they passed the time eating and

talking about Johnny and his kids, Jennifer and her troubles, and Aunt Lillian's restaurant. When Sadie asked, Truman told her about his older brother Kennedy and Kennedy's three boys. They avoided all talk of the body Sadie had found that afternoon.

As their waitress placed dessert on the table, cheesecake and coffee, an awkward silence fell. They'd run out of safe things to talk about.

"So," Sadie said, flicking a fork at the strawberry topping on her cheesecake. "How's your knee?"

Truman's jaw tightened. A tiny muscle in his eyelid twitched. Talk about a mood killer. Murder was a more pleasant subject. He didn't talk about the old injury, not anymore. No one mentioned the limp, not even on those damp mornings when he couldn't hide the pain. No one asked him about the old days. And he didn't much like thinking about what might have been. What a waste of time that was.

"It's fine," he said, his voice low.

Sadie wasn't going to take *fine* for an answer, she wasn't going to let him off that easy. "What bullshit," she said succinctly.

"Language, Sadie Mae."

"Don't try to change the subject by calling me Sadie Mae and getting me all riled up. It won't work this time."

He looked her in the eye. He hadn't done that often, this evening. "You want to know how my knee is? Hamburger. My freakin' knee is hamburger. I can't run, climbing stairs is a bitch and some mornings it hurts like hell just to get out of bed." She wanted to know, he might as well tell her everything. "I'm a thirty-three-year-old gimp whose glory days came and went before he was twenty-five. A divorced gimp, whose wife left because when she màrried him she had her sights set on the money and fame that came with being married to a professional quarterback. A small-town deputy wasn't exactly what she had in mind. She wanted Joe Montana and ended up with a gimpy Barney Fife. That's how my damn knee is."

Sadie didn't look away, as he'd suspected she might. She didn't glance down and break the hold his eyes had on hers and start mumbling about something safe, like the weather. "I knew it wasn't *fine*," she said.

"I don't want to talk about my knee," he said. "I don't want to talk about myself at all. Your life is much more interesting than mine."

She dumped a pack of sugar into her coffee and stirred absently. With a tilt of her head and a sigh, she looked a little bit like the girl he remembered. Not so tough, after all. "Let's change the subject," she said softly.

"Gladly."

"What do you know about Aidan Hearn? Was he into anything dirty, like drugs or money laundering?"

"We can't be having this conversation, Sadie."

"I'm not asking about anything that might've come up in the investigation. I'm interested in gossip, that's all. I could ask anyone else in town."

"But you're asking me."

"You're here," she said softly, and the way her mouth wrapped around the words… Yeah, she was definitely messing with his head.

"Far as I know, Hearn was clean as a whistle. No drugs, no money laundering." He almost snorted. Had she forgotten what Garth was like? "I have heard rumors over the years that he was a bit of a ladies' man, but…"

"I thought he was married."

"He is."

Sadie's eyes positively sparkled. "Why did Evans even bother talking to me? The wife, a girlfriend, an ex-girlfriend…if Hearn wasn't into something dirty, then the murder was personal."

"You're probably right."

"So…"

"I thought we weren't going to talk about this," Truman interrupted.

She looked him in the eye, smiled and shrugged. "Sorry. Occupational hazard."

Why did he know in his gut that this woman was trouble? That she found or created trouble wherever she went? She settled back in her chair for a moment and again let her gaze travel about the room. This time her mind was definitely elsewhere. More trouble.

He insisted on paying for dinner, and while Sadie argued, she eventually backed off. A rarity for her, he imagined.

"How about a short drive before I take you back to the motel?" he asked as he opened the door of his pickup truck for her.

"I don't know," she said, stepping onto the runner, pulling her great legs into the truck. "It's been a long day."

"I have a quick errand to run. Won't take but a few minutes," he promised.

"Okay."

* * *

Miranda Lake. How many babies had been conceived in cars parked along the edge of the lake? Plenty, Sadie suspected. In Garth and the surrounding area, there was an unnatural number of baby girls named Miranda born every year.

"What are we doing here?" she asked suspiciously. She'd specifically told Truman she wasn't interested in sleeping with him, and even if she were…she was a little old to get lucky in a pickup truck.

"Nightly patrol," he said. "I'm off duty, but since I live close by I usually make a nightly drive through. There are half a dozen or so spots where the teenagers park, and every night I hit one or two of them. Keeps the kiddies on their toes." He turned a corner, and sure enough, there were four cars parked in the gravel lot that looked over Miranda Lake. He pulled into a parking space of his own, smiled at Sadie and told her he'd be right back then stepped out of the truck. Almost immediately, three engines came to life. Truman smiled and waved at the teenagers who made their escape, and walked toward the one remaining car. The occupants were obviously too engrossed to know they'd been caught.

Sadie watched Truman walk away. Yeah, maybe there was a little bit of a hitch in his step, but he was far from a gimp. That ex-wife of his was a real bitch, to leave him when he needed her most, to run out when he was already hurting. She'd never met the woman, but she had seen pictures. Even then, from a mere photograph, Sadie had known the woman Truman married right out of college wasn't good enough for him. Then again, maybe she would have thought the same about any woman Truman married.

Why did Truman stay in Garth? Sure, his mother was here, and he had old friends in town, but... She had always known Truman McCain was meant for greater things, that he was meant for greater places than Garth, Alabama. She hated to think that he might be hiding here, staying because it was safe, because he would always be a hero to the locals for getting out and making it big; even if his escape and his fame hadn't lasted.

He leaned down and tapped on a steamed-up window. After a moment where all was still and quiet, the window rolled down. Truman said a few soft words, and the engine revved to life. He stepped back, and the last car made a quick getaway.

After the kids were gone, Truman headed back to the pickup where Sadie waited.

"What a job," she said with a grin.

"When the mayor found out his daughter had been coming out here with her new boyfriend, we had to step up patrols." He settled into the driver's seat and looked out over the water. "It is a beautiful place," he added softly.

"You said you live close by," Sadie said.

Truman rested his arm on the steering wheel and pointed to the other side of the lake. "I have a cabin over there. Small, but nice, and it looks out over the water. What else does a man need?"

The question hung in the air, unanswered.

Sadie rested her head on the seat and stared out over the water. Moonlight sparkled there, gentle waves lapped. "Did you ever wonder if the story was true?" she asked, her voice soft to match the mood and the night.

"What story?"

"About Miranda Fairchild and Samuel Garth."

"The ghosts," Truman deadpanned. "Some old tale about a couple of ancient people who killed themselves. I don't know what it is chicks like about that story."

Sadie sighed. "You never got laid out here, did you?"

"I got laid out here plenty, and I never had to resort to ghost stories to get what I wanted."

Of course he hadn't. Gorgeous football hero with a killer smile, all Truman had to do was grin, and he got whatever he wanted. It was so unfair.

"It's a beautiful story." Heavens, she was tired. But this was nice, resting her head against the seat, looking out over the water, talking to Truman.

"Okay, convince me. What happened, exactly?" Truman prodded.

Sadie took her eyes from the moonlit water, for a moment. No, he wasn't teasing her. At least, he looked serious. Maybe it was a fanciful story, more legend than fact, but there was something mesmerizing about the tale. At least, there once had been. Living with Spencer had killed most of Sadie's fanciful notions about love and happily ever after. There was no forever. A man would always get tired of a woman. He'd get bored and go elsewhere looking for love, no matter how hard she tried to make him happy.

Reality was harsh. No wonder a touch of fantasy, a tale of romance, seemed so attractive at the moment.

"When Samuel was called to the war with those nasty Yankees, he and Miranda wanted to get married." Not a wise choice, in Sadie's estimation, but she tried to push away her own bad experience and just enjoy the story.

"They wanted to be together before he left, but Miranda's father said she was too young. She was sixteen. Samuel was a couple of years older. Eighteen or nineteen, maybe. Since her father refused to allow them to marry, Miranda swore she'd wait for Samuel. She said she'd wait forever, if she had to."

Truman shook his head in disbelief, and Sadie returned her gaze to the water. "So Samuel went to war," she said softly. "You know how it was. They all thought the unpleasantness with the Yankees would last weeks. Months, maybe. But Samuel was gone for years. When word came that he'd died in battle, Miranda very calmly left her house, walked to the lake, and drowned herself."

"Stupid," Truman muttered.

"You do not have a romantic bone in your body."

"Only the one."

Sadie sighed, holding in a laugh. "You're hopeless."

"Yes, ma'am."

"Anyway," Sadie continued, determined to finish. "Grieving and desolate, Miranda drowned. A year to the day later, Samuel comes home expecting to find his love waiting for him. He hadn't been killed in battle after all."

"Obviously."

Sadie cleared her throat to chastise him for interrupting. "When he discovers what happened to Miranda he walks to the lake, swims out as far as he can, and then goes under, never to be seen again."

"He killed himself, just like she did. I still say that's not…"

"Would you hush," Sadie said, laughing lightly. "You're ruining the story."

"Excuse me," he said insincerely.

"After that night, it was said that sometimes when there was a full moon people would see them in the lake and on the shore, making love at last, together forever."

Forever. Nice idea. Too bad it was a crock.

"And this ridiculous story actually gets people laid." Truman shook his head.

"Oh, you know that tale as well as I do."

"Yeah, I just wanted to hear you tell it." He smiled softly. "So, who told it to you?"

Sadie closed her eyes and took a deep breath. "Jason Davenport. Prom night, thirteen years ago."

"Jason *Davenport?*"

Jason Davenport. Running back for the high-school football team. First baseman for the baseball team. Black hair, green eyes, and oh, he had a really great voice. She could still hear him telling that story to her, reminding her that there wouldn't always be a tomorrow, that they'd better take what they wanted tonight. "Yeah."

"I didn't even know you dated that guy."

"Just a couple of times. Then he dumped me." The fuzzy memories faded. As soon as Jason realized he wasn't going to get what he wanted, he'd quit calling. Jerk. She should have learned her lesson then.

"He's still around, you know."

"Really?"

"Yeah, he's some kind of artist or something," Truman said grudgingly. "You actually…" he stopped, choked on the word.

"It's ancient history," Sadie said, not wanting to answer him either way. Oh, it was so quiet out here! Quiet and beautiful, peaceful in a way she had forgotten. Gentle wind lapped at the water and ruffled the leaves of trees surrounding the lake. If the breeze hit the trees just right, it sounded as if a woman moaned. Soft. Happy. Miranda. Sadie took a deep breath and inhaled the scent of the lake.

Okay, so Garth wasn't a complete loss. It had Aunt Lillian's biscuits, Miranda Lake and Truman. Individually they weren't much, but when you put them all together…maybe it was a nice place to be, for a while.

Chapter 3

She hadn't slept this deeply in months. Years, maybe! Sadie sighed and fought the awareness that crept upon her. She didn't want to wake up. She needed more of this dreamless sleep. The quiet. The warmth. The rest for her bone-weary body and agitated mind.

A soft spring wind ruffled the leaves of a tree, water lapped. Truman shifted his body and dropped a hand into her hair. His thigh was her pillow, and there was a little spot of drool, right there on the denim that was stretched over that thigh.

"Oh, crap," Sadie muttered, immediately awake and shooting up into a semi-sitting position. Her fingers rubbed against the wet spot on Truman's thigh, trying to erase the evidence. All her efforts managed to do was wake Truman.

For a moment he smiled at her, then he realized where they were and his smile faded. "Damn," he muttered.

"Exactly." Sadie straightened the strap of her bra. Everything she wore was twisted and misshapen at the moment. "What time is it?"

Truman checked his watch, hitting a button on the side to light the face. He squinted, blinked twice. "Four-thirty."

Almost instinctively, she reached out and slapped Truman on the arm. "Why did you let me sleep in your pickup truck until four-thirty? Jennifer will have the whole town out looking for us. I was supposed to be home by ten."

"Ten?" Truman shook his head. "You're thirty years old, for God's sake. Why did you have to be home by ten?"

"*Almost* thirty," she corrected. "And I said I'd be home by ten so Jennifer could go out." It really wasn't a disaster. Jen would survive. Sadie ran her fingers through her hair. So much for her careful attempts at styling the mop. It was going every which a way, as it usually did in the morning. "Go, go," she said with a wave of her hand.

Truman started the engine and put the truck in Reverse, yawning and then working a crick out of his neck. A very fine neck, she had to admit. Sadie stared at him. So, this was what Truman McCain looked like in the morning. Rumpled. Sexy as hell. It just wasn't fair.

"Why did you let me sleep?" she asked, trying for anger but delivering sheer frustration.

"You were exhausted. I figured a few minutes wouldn't hurt." Truman steered the truck down the narrow drive that would take them back to the main road, headlights dancing in the morning dark.

"A few minutes?"

He grinned, the rat. "Then I fell asleep. Long day. Sorry."

Sadie ran her fingers through her hair again, trying to tame the curls. Four-thirty. Almost time for Mary Beth and Aunt Lillian and Bowie to get to work. No one else would be out at this hour of the morning but for a few fishermen whose minds were on bait and boats and elusive bass. She could sneak up to her room and no one would ever be the wiser, except for Jennifer. And Jen could be persuaded to keep her mouth shut. Blackmail between cousins was a wonderful thing.

Truman glanced over and down and grinned sleepily. "Found it."

"What?"

"You said I wouldn't."

Sadie realized he was staring at her mostly bare leg and her thigh holster. She yanked her skirt down to cover the leather and the pistol housed there. "Drop me off at the side door of the lobby."

"Where no one can see you from the street?" Truman teased.

"Exactly." She shot him an accusing glance. "And stop smiling! This isn't funny."

"Sure it is," he said half-heartedly.

"I should've met you at the restaurant," Sadie said beneath her breath. "I have my own car. I could have gone straight home when dinner was finished and this never would've happened."

"Now, where's the fun in that?" Truman asked, his Southern accent deepening as he teased her.

It wasn't a long trip from Miranda Lake to the Yellow Rose Motel. Seven minutes, tops. Ten at what passed as rush hour in the small town. There was no traffic this early in the morning, but Truman insisted on driving the speed limit, which was ridiculously slow. Finally, Sadie saw the motel sign. Home, for the time being. The neon sign for Lillian's Café wasn't lit up yet. That meant Lillian wasn't in. Good. Sadie figured she had about two minutes to make it to the safety of her room without being seen.

Truman pulled into the parking lot, and Sadie's heart sank. There sat a patrol car, lights flashing. A young deputy leaned against the fender, taking notes and nodding his head, while Jennifer spoke and gestured wildly with her hands. Either someone else had gotten themselves killed at the Yellow Rose or Jennifer had actually called the sheriff's office to report her cousin missing.

Instead of driving to the side door as Sadie as asked—which would have been a waste of time, given the circumstances—Truman pulled his truck alongside the patrol car and rolled down his window.

"Bryce," he said with a nod of his head. "What's up?"

Bryce, who even though he was at least six feet tall looked to be about twelve years old, snapped his notebook shut. "I was just telling Jennifer that I couldn't fill out a missing persons report on her cousin just yet." He leaned down a little bit farther, set his eyes on Sadie, and grinned. "You must be Sadie Mae." He glanced at Jennifer. "I told you if your cousin was with Truman she'd be just fine."

Jennifer crossed her arms and glared at Sadie through the windshield, a picture of pouting petulance in her tight jeans and cropped shirt that showed off her belly button and the shiny silver ring that sparkled there. Sadie stared at the piercing for a moment. Didn't it *hurt?*

Truman waggled his fingers at the young deputy. "I think you can turn off your lights now. The emergency is over."

The kid reached into his patrol car and shut off the flashing lights, but not before accidentally giving the sirens a quick wail.

So much for a quick, quiet return home. Sadie threw open her door and stepped into the parking lot. Immediately, Truman killed the engine and followed suit.

She stood and looked at him over the hood of his truck. "You really don't have to escort me to the door," she said dryly.

He continued to walk around the truck, limping more than usual. Sleeping in the truck couldn't be good for his knee. Dammit, she refused, absolutely *refused,* to worry about his knee like she cared about him and whether or not he hurt.

"It was fun," he said. "We'll have to do it again."

Sadie shook her head. No way. This one evening had been bad enough, and there would be no repeat performance.

Jennifer stalked toward her. "How could you do this to me? I was worried sick. Ten. You said ten!"

"Sorry," Sadie said, anxious to make her getaway before anyone else saw her.

"Sorry," Jennifer said, once again crossing her arms across her chest. "That hardly seems sufficient."

Bryce and Truman both laughed.

Sadie stared at Truman, at his sleepy blue eyes that

had an unexpected crinkle at the corner. "What's so funny?"

"You don't know how many nights we went out looking for your little cousin before she turned eighteen."

"That was different," Jennifer said, blushing a bright red. "Sadie's old enough to know better!"

Jennifer's eyes dropped slightly, and her mouth pursed in obvious disapproval. Unable to help herself, Sadie followed those eyes. Right next to the little slobber spot on Truman's jeans was a smudge of red lipstick. "This isn't what it looks like," she said softly.

Jennifer shook her head like a wearied parent and raised her accusing eyes to Sadie. She continued to shake her head. "You're missing an earring."

Both hands flew up to check earlobes. Sure enough, the left lobe was bare. "I can't believe I lost one of those diamond studs."

"I'm pretty sure you had them both when we left the restaurant," Truman said calmly. "It's probably in the truck."

"You can look for it later," Sadie said, backing up a step toward the hotel. "No rush." The earrings had cost her a small fortune, a gift to herself when she'd gotten her last raise, but no amount of money was worth prolonging this torture.

But Bryce was already leaning into the driver's side of the truck, dutifully checking the seat cushions. He found the earring in a matter of seconds. "Here it is," he said, coming up with something in his hand. "Half of it, anyway."

The good half, Sadie saw as the young deputy offered her the diamond on the palm of his hand.

"It was wedged there in the cushion of the, uh, driver's seat."

The earring had probably come loose while she'd slept with her head in Truman's lap. Jennifer and Bryce obviously thought other things had been going on, in the, uh, driver's seat.

"Thank you." Sadie saw no reason to offer explanations. Anything she said would just sound like a pathetic excuse at this point.

Truman came toward her, favoring his right leg, smiling like this was all so very amusing. He looked freshly tumbled, warm and sleepy and…happy. If she looked anything like this, no wonder Bryce grinned like an idiot and Jen frowned and shook her head.

"It was great," Truman said softly, but plenty loud enough for the others to hear.

"Nothing was great," Sadie insisted. "There was no great."

"How about Friday?" he asked, his voice a touch lower than before.

"Not on your life," she whispered.

A car door slammed. Mary Beth had arrived at the coffee shop. The waitress glanced at the commotion in the parking lot, smiled and headed for the front door with her key in hand. Bowie was right beside her. They whispered and giggled as they entered the café.

Sadie sighed. Had she actually thought her return home might be quiet and uneventful?

"There you are!" A familiar voice called from behind. Sadie closed her eyes as Aunt Lillian approached. "I don't need you for breakfast today," the woman continued. "But I will need you for lunch."

"Sure," Sadie said without turning to look at her aunt.

"Would you two like breakfast? We'll be open in a few minutes."

Sadie looked her aunt in the eye, and saw that in spite of her casual voice and smile she'd been crying. Still or again? A murder taking place so close by obviously had shaken her.

"I'm starving," Truman said.

"I'm not hungry," Sadie countered. "Not at all."

Lillian stopped and laid a hand on Sadie's arm and another on Truman's. "You two make such a cute couple," she said with a wan smile.

"Thank you," Truman said.

"We do not!" Sadie insisted.

The older woman moved on, unperturbed.

Sadie glared at Truman. "Don't you have to go to work or something?"

"I'm off today."

"Well, I'm not." Sadie turned and walked toward the lobby and the stairs that would take her up to her own room where she could hide for a while.

Behind her another car door slammed, and Sadie cringed. Time for the café to open, and there was no telling who that was. Someone called a friendly greeting to Truman, and he answered as if this were all perfectly natural.

"Sadie," Truman called as she reached the lobby doors.

She stopped, hesitated, and then turned to face him. He was still smiling, but not quite so brightly. "You look good in the morning. Really good."

Jennifer joined Sadie and slapped her cousin on the

arm as Truman turned away. "Told you," she said softly. "I never should have let you leave here wearing those shoes."

The ABI still had room 119 cordoned off with yellow tape, which Aunt Lillian insisted was scaring away her customers. They had promised to have it down by this afternoon, but wanted Lillian to keep the room untouched in case they needed to go back in. No problem. Who would want to rent that room, anyway? Sadie shuddered at the thought, and she was not a woman who shuddered easily or often.

There was still no sign of Conrad. He hadn't shown up for work last night, and there was no sign of him at home. Unfortunately that didn't mean much. He was an unreliable employee who worked just enough to support his beer and fishing habits. His absence didn't necessarily mean he was in danger. But Sadie didn't like the timing of his disappearance. Not at all.

The ABI investigator interrogated her for a second time, and she answered all his questions truthfully. Evans assumed that she worked with the family all the time, and since he didn't ask about her profession, she didn't feel the need to tell him. Some cops had a real hard spot for PIs, and all she wanted was to get out of this mess as quickly and cleanly as possible. If he went so far as to run a check on her, he'd find everything. Working for Benning wasn't illegal or immoral, in spite of Lillian's horror at her niece's chosen profession, and Sadie hadn't gone to great lengths to conceal anything. Evans just hadn't asked the right questions, and that wasn't her fault.

Sadie could read people pretty well. Evans didn't really suspect her of murder, but as far as she could see he wasn't looking elsewhere. He really wanted to talk to Conrad, though as far as Sadie knew there was absolutely no connection between the banker and the part-time motel clerk who'd disappeared. When she got the chance she'd do a little investigating of her own. Finding the killer wasn't her job, but she was curious.

She reminded herself of what curiosity had done to the cat, but the self-warning did no good. The victim in 119 was, in a way, her body. She'd found it. Finders keepers and all that.

No matter what had happened, she was expected to work lunch at Aunt Lillian's. Uncomfortable or not, she decided to wear the thigh holster when she couldn't hide the shoulder holster. And as she donned the dreaded pink uniform, she once again dropped the knife into her pocket.

Even in Garth, apparently, a woman couldn't be too careful.

This was without a doubt the most foolish thing he'd done in a very long time. Truman McCain didn't take chances. Not anymore.

Eating lunch at Lillian's Café on Wednesday was most definitely taking a chance. What the hell had gotten into him?

That. *That* had gotten into him. He watched Sadie as she perched on a stool at the counter, her ghastly uniform hanging shapelessly on what he knew to be a great body, one very nice leg rocking gently. If she'd offered herself to him last night, the way she had when she'd been sixteen, would he be thinking about her all the time? Probably not. She tells him she won't sleep with him, and suddenly that's all he can think about. Sleeping with Sadie.

"Hey," he called.

Sadie spun around on her stool. "Have patience, mister," she said with a smile. "I'll be right with you. This is the lunch rush, you know."

Truman scanned the empty café quickly. He was the only customer. Five days out of the week, this popular place was packed for lunch. Sundays it was closed. But on Wednesday the special was Lillian's Gelatin Surprise. And if you came to Lillian's Café for lunch, you ate the special. No burgers, no soup or hotdogs. It was like going to your grandmother's for lunch. You ate what was served or you ate somewhere else.

After making him wait another five minutes, Sadie sauntered his way. The decent night's sleep in his truck looked good on her. She wasn't as tired as she'd been yesterday. Her dark eyes sparkled.

She stopped beside his booth, cocked her hip out, and held a sharp pencil poised over the order pad.

"I'll have the special," Truman said, the words low as they escaped through his clenched teeth.

She actually wrote it down. "And to drink?"

"Tea. Sweet."

Again, she wrote carefully, as if she were juggling a dozen orders.

She was doing this to him on purpose. Torturing him. Teasing him. He really should just get up and walk out and forget her altogether.

He didn't. He watched Sadie walk away, letting the sway of her hips ease his frustration…and then add to it.

It had been too long since he'd had a woman, that's why she grated on his nerves this way. He'd avoided anything resembling a relationship since coming back to Garth, but that didn't mean he lived like a monk. Still, it had been a while. It had been months. That's why Sadie looked so damned good.

She was back moments later, a huge glass of iced tea in one hand, a jiggling plate of Lillian's Gelatin Surprise in the other. She carefully placed them both before him. But instead of walking away as he expected, she stayed put, a half smile on her face and a sexy cant to her hip as she waited.

Truman glanced down at his plate. He'd never actually eaten here on Wednesday before. The warnings from others who had been brave enough or hungry enough to confront the Wednesday special had been enough. And he didn't really want to know what the "surprise" was.

He poked a fork at the jiggling green mass on his plate. Was that…broccoli? Inside the lime gelatin? And…sausage? Surely not.

Sadie stayed put, her smile gradually growing.

Truman put his fork aside and glanced up at her. "Have you ever suggested that your aunt serve spaghetti on Wednesday? Or meat loaf? Or…anything but *this?*"

"Yeah. Me and half the town."

"Why doesn't she?"

Sadie placed her hands on her table and leaned down. "She plays bridge on Wednesday afternoon. This way she's sure to get out of here early."

"She can't just hire someone else to close up?"

Sadie shook her head. "Doesn't trust anyone else with the job, not even her own daughter. Said she left Jennifer here by herself once and she almost burned the place down. Mary Beth has her hands full working breakfast six days a week, and she's got three kids that her mother keeps until eleven, but then her mother has a job at the dry cleaners…"

"Fine," Truman snapped. "I get it."

Someone else, a poor unsuspecting hungry person, came through the front door and made his way to the counter.

"You have another customer," Truman said with a wag of his fork.

"Aunt Lillian watches the counter."

Truman glanced up sharply. "Why the sudden undivided attention?"

"Just trying to earn my tip from yesterday," she said sweetly.

He stabbed at the gelatin. Maybe that red thing floating in there was the "surprise." "You just want to watch me eat this, don't you?"

"Yeah," she said, her smile growing so wide he couldn't make himself look away.

"Fine," he said. If he didn't eat the absurd and wiggling green mass on his plate, Sadie would know he was only here because *she* was here. She surely suspected that was the case, but he didn't want her to be certain. She was already stringing him along, and doing a fine job of it.

"It just so happens that I love surprises," he said as he forked up a small portion of the gelatin.

"Good to know," Sadie said softly.

Truman held his breath while he shoveled the gelatin mess into his mouth. Maybe if he didn't breathe he could swallow without making a face that would give him away.

He swallowed, then gestured to the seat across from him. "You're not busy. Why don't you get a plate and join me?"

"I don't eat that stuff," Sadie said, maintaining her stance beside him. "Besides, it's not a good idea to fraternize with the customers."

"One of Lillian's rules?"

"One of my rules."

Truman took another bite. The gelatin surprise wasn't actually as bad as it looked, but it wasn't good, either. "Why doesn't Lillian just close up after breakfast on Wednesdays?" he asked when he'd swallowed the second bite.

"And let her customers go hungry?" Sadie smiled, then she stifled a laugh.

"Snorting at the customers. How attractive." Truman shook his head. "This makes no sense. How can she be worried about her customers? No one's here, but me and that poor unsuspecting guy at the counter."

"Hey, if you can reason with Aunt Lillian, have at it. I can't, and neither can anyone else in the family." Sadie shrugged. "Jennifer doesn't even try anymore. Aunt Lillian does what she wants."

The guy at the counter took one look at his "surprise" and left.

Truman poked at his gelatin. How low had he fallen?

How freakin' desperate was he? "So, what are you doing Friday night?" he asked.

"Nothing," Sadie answered quickly.

"Want to…"

"I told you before, no," she said. Her smile was gone, her easy posture changed rapidly. "It's not a good idea."

"It's a very good idea," he countered.

She didn't have any intention of answering. She'd said no. That was that. He really should just let it go.

"About Friday…"

"Truman, just give it up. It's not going to happen."

God, she was stubborn! He lowered his voice. "Please tell me you're not harboring a grudge because I wouldn't sleep with my best friend's cousin when she was barely sixteen years old."

"That's ridiculous," she whispered.

"I know!"

They both stopped speaking when Lillian Banks came toward them carrying a tray bearing a pitcher of tea, an extra glass and a plate of…bless her soul…sandwiches.

"I'm closing up early," Lillian said. "Here's your lunch, Sadie," she said, expertly placing everything she carried on Truman's table. "I'll lock up, but you two can let yourselves out when you're finished. Spare key's under the register."

Truman pointed at Sadie's plate. "Why doesn't Sadie get the surprise?"

"She doesn't like it," Lillian said with a shake of her gray head. "And it's a woman's God-given duty to spoil her family."

Explanation enough for Lillian Banks. She walked

away, her step hurried, exited the coffee shop, and locked the door behind her.

Sadie took her seat on the padded bench opposite Truman and picked up half a sandwich. She offered it to him at the end of an outstretched arm. "Lillian knows darn well I'm not going to sit here and eat three sandwiches. I guess she thinks you need to put a little meat on those bones."

"She thinks we're a cute couple," Truman said as he took the sandwich.

Sadie's grin widened. "She also thinks Lawrence Welk is the cat's pajamas."

"Lawrence Welk?" Truman said. "Shouldn't she be into Mick Jagger or Paul McCartney?"

"Lillian's mother was a big musical influence in her life."

There was no arguing with Sadie. Truman pushed away the gelatin surprise, and gratefully ate the sandwich. He washed it down with sweet iced tea, and when the gelatin called to him, he scooped up the plate and deposited it on a nearby table where it was out of sight.

Every now and then he caught Sadie looking at him as if she felt the same attraction he did. It couldn't be his imagination that sparks made the air heavier. Electric. Maybe it was strictly physical…maybe it was just his hopeful imagination. Sparks were for kids. This feeling of standing on the edge of something new and exciting, ready to jump or fall…he'd outgrown that feeling years ago.

But he really would like to get Sadie naked. Just once.

Lunch was finished, they had the place to themselves. Truman laid his forearms on the table and leaned slightly toward Sadie. "Friday…"

"No."

"Saturday, then…"

"I'm not going out with you, McCain. We tried it once, it didn't work."

"I thought it worked just fine."

Her eyes darkened, and there was no longer even a hint of a smile on her pretty face. "I disagree."

Enough was enough. Sadie didn't want to have anything to do with him, fine. Maybe it was some old grudge. Then again maybe she simply didn't like him anymore and the attraction he was so sure she shared was strictly one-sided.

He rose and reached for his wallet at the same time, ready to pay and get out of here.

"On the house," Sadie said. "You earned it," she said, glancing at the gelatin surprise.

"No." Truman stood beside the table and took out a ten-dollar bill. "Keep the change."

"No way."

He wasn't going through this again. He carried the ten to the register, popped open the drawer, and dropped in the bill. Then he went looking for the spare key.

His fingers brushed bare counter, so he bent down to take a closer look. No key. "Sadie, where's the key?"

"Very funny."

He straightened up and saw that she was walking toward him. "No joke. It's not here."

Sadie didn't believe him, she had to see for herself. She came behind the counter and bent down to look beneath the register. The counter was clean and bare.

"I'll call the main desk. Jennifer is on this afternoon.

She'll know where Lillian is, and she can call and get her back over here to let us out."

"Good."

"She might even have a spare key there in the office." Ah, the gleam of hope in her eyes…

All Sadie had to do was turn and reach for the phone. She dialed the number, then quickly and simply told her cousin what had happened. Truman could hear the laughter through the receiver from where he stood.

"Jen, I swear…" Sadie said in response to her cousin's laughter. She stopped abruptly, looked down at the receiver in her hand, and then banged it down.

"I take it Jennifer is not running to the rescue," Truman said tightly.

"Nope. This is our repayment for making her stay home last night. She said Aunt Lillian will be back about five."

"Great. What about the back door?" He turned without waiting for an answer, and pushed his way through the door that led to the kitchen and beyond.

Sadie followed. "Forget it. Aunt Lillian got tired of the short-order cooks going out to smoke and then not locking up when they came back in. She put on a…"

Truman lifted the lock before Sadie could tell him why they couldn't slip out the back.

"Padlock," she finished quietly. "She carries the key in her purse."

"I'm pretty sure this is a fire-code violation," he said as he stared at the padlock. "At least during business hours." Truman turned and leaned against the back door. Trapped. At least until five. Could be worse. They had food, plenty to drink, a couple of bathrooms…and in three hours or so Lillian would be here with her spare key.

"We could break a window," Sadie said. She glanced up. "And there's probably roof access underneath those ceiling tiles. If we can't find a ladder, I'll stand on your shoulders and…"

"Let's look around and see if we can't find the spare key first," Truman suggested calmly. "I have a feeling the two of us breaking a window or going through the roof to get out of here is going to give the town something to talk about."

"Like they aren't already talking," Sadie said dismally.

"I don't like this any more than you do." He brushed past her, headed for the front counter.

"Maybe if we stand in the window and look really sad and desperate, someone will see us and Jen will be forced to call Aunt Lillian."

Truman spun on her. He'd had enough. A few words from Sadie pushed him beyond his reserve of patience. Like a cautious turtle he sticks his head out for the first time in years, and what happens? Sadie Harlow threatens to take it off.

"Sad and desperate? Is that how a couple of hours locked in here with me makes you feel? Sad and *desperate?*"

He expected her to deny it, to respond with something light and funny, something pithy to immediately remind him that he was overreacting.

She didn't.

"Yeah."

Chapter 4

She didn't panic, not ever, and if she ever did it wouldn't be over something silly like this. So why was her heart beating too fast? Why did her mouth taste like copper? Locked in Aunt Lillian's café with Truman, nowhere to go, zilch to do but pretend she found him nothing more than an amusing nuisance. In the past few years she'd been in much more dire circumstances, and here she was almost in a frenzy...

The frenzy faded in a rush. "Mary Beth," Sadie said, closing her eyes and breathing deep in relief. "She has a key."

"Good," Truman's response was low and rumbling. A man's voice, not the voice of the boy she'd loved a very long time ago. No, not *loved*. Lusted after. Wanted. Drooled over. That wasn't love. She just hadn't known that at the age of fifteen, where every new emotion was intense and life-altering.

Sadie found the directory near the phone, leafed through the pages of the thin book, and laid her finger on Mary Beth Baxter's number. She dialed quickly. Mary Beth could be trusted. She'd let them out, and if they asked nicely she wouldn't blab the amusing story about Sadie Harlow and Truman McCain getting themselves locked in the café to everyone in town. Sadie was willing to pay big to see that Mary Beth kept quiet. After this morning, there was probably enough gossip to keep the town going for a while.

The phone on the other end rang. What if Mary Beth wasn't home? Sadie's heart started to pound again. Finally, someone picked up, and for a half second Sadie felt a rush of relief. Then a cheery voice chimed, "Hi! We're not home right now. Leave a message at the…"

Sadie slammed down the phone.

"Nobody home?" Truman, who stood to close behind her, asked.

"Answering machine."

Sadie turned and faced him. She could really panic and call a locksmith or bust through a window, giving the entire town yet another topic of gossip, or she could settle in and wait for Aunt Lillian to get back. She didn't have to worry about Jennifer not telling her mother to let them out until morning. If Sadie was locked up all night, Jennifer would have to stay home and work. They'd be stuck here for a few hours, that was all. Surely she could handle that.

Truman offered a suggestion of his own. "I can call the sheriff's office and have them…"

"No," Sadie interrupted sharply. She took a deep breath and calmed herself. "A parking lot full of patrol cars is just going to draw attention to the…the situation." She had planned to visit Hearn's secretary this afternoon. Well, she was likely some other bank official's secretary now, but still…Rhea something-or-another, that was her name. She was one of those bubble-headed blondes who spent more time and energy on her nails and her hair than her brain, and if Sadie pushed just the right buttons she'd spill everything about her late boss's personal life.

Yeah, she'd much rather think about murder than her current situation.

Truman leaned against the counter and gave her a smile. "Are you really that worried about what people think? About what they say? Who cares?"

She'd tried to embrace that attitude in the past few years. Life was so much easier when you didn't care what anyone thought of you. But this was Garth, the scene of so many of her young mistakes. She had family here, and like it or not she did care about her family's opinion. Lillian and Jen were off-center, unconventional and stubborn. But they were all she had.

She'd lived with her mother for eleven years, but when she thought of home it was here. Sadie and her mother had moved a lot, from one apartment to another, to a trailer or two, to a house with that one man who'd promised to marry the widow and make her daughter his own. That hadn't worked out either.

No, Garth was the only home she'd ever known. That didn't mean she wanted to stay, but still…to imagine the people here laughing about her predicament was more than she could handle, at the moment. If that made her juvenile and petty, so be it.

Sadie headed for the kitchen. Surely there was something in the place that needed cleaning. Something she could scrub for a couple of hours.

Truman followed her. "You came home to help your family when they needed you. That's a good thing, Sadie."

"It doesn't feel so good at the moment," she admitted in a low voice.

"Because Hearn ended up dead or because I'm here?"

Sadie turned and leaned against a spotless kitchen counter, and for the first time she allowed herself to see Truman as he really was. Not her cousin's best friend, not the football hero, not the guy who'd laughed at her thirteen and a half years ago when she'd tried to seduce him. All that was past. Here and now he was just a nice guy who had tried very hard to be good to her. He was sweet and good-looking and charming and sexy…and all she'd done was give him grief.

"Not because you're here," she said softly.

But one thing hadn't changed. She could not fall for Truman, any more than she could fall for any other man in Garth. She was nothing in this little town that felt like home. In this place she didn't have a chance to be anything but waitress and maid and desk clerk.

"Are you happy here?" she asked.

Truman cocked his head to one side. "Most of the time."

"Why?"

He leaned against the doorjamb, casual and unexpectedly appealing in his jeans and forest-green shirt. "It's not very exciting, I know, but I like living in a place where I know everyone and they know me, where you can count on your neighbors, where the fishing is good." He grinned. "I like living my life where the year's greatest excitement comes from a bass festival and the accompanying craft fair. It's quiet and real and good here, most of the time."

"Don't you miss..." she began, and the words stuck in her throat. What a stupid question. Of course he did! He'd been in the limelight for a while, he'd lived every man's dream...for a while.

"Sometimes," he answered softly. "Not very often." He shifted his feet, crossed his arms over his chest. "You don't like it here."

"I don't know if I like it or not."

"So why are you so anxious to get out of town?"

Because I might start to feel like this is home again. Maybe I already have. "I need to get on with my life. I have a really great career with Benning. I'm good at what I do."

"I don't doubt it." He studied her carefully, like a man accustomed to sizing people up with a glance.

Whatever the reason for the way he looked at her, the examination made Sadie shiver a little.

"Did a man hurt you?" Truman asked sharply. "Is that the reason you're so skittish?"

"I'm not skittish," she said defensively.

"You're about to come out of your skin."

For a period of time, a few months, maybe a year or two, she'd truly thought Spencer Mayfield was her Samuel Garth. She'd looked at him and seen forever. She'd fallen for all of his lies and seen the end of the rainbow, her own happily ever after. What a crock. She'd worked hard at making their relationship work, and still he'd gotten bored with her. Bored! Making love to her had become a chore to him, an obligation. She'd spent years wondering what was wrong with her. She still wondered…but she couldn't tell Truman any of that.

"I made mistakes. We all know what that's like. But it was years ago and I was different, then." Needy. Always worried. Living at the whims of a man who didn't love her. "I don't love him anymore. If I met Spencer today, I wouldn't even like him."

"That's not exactly what I was asking, but it'll do. For now."

Sadie couldn't pretend that there was anything left in the café to clean. The place sparkled. What was left of Aunt Lillian's Gelatin Surprise had gone down the disposal. The sight of that gelatinous mess disappearing down the drain had given Truman reason to worry about the water system in Garth.

"What time is it?" Sadie asked, not for the first time in the past half hour.

"Three-fourteen," he answered.

She nodded slowly and headed for the phone to try Mary Beth again.

"She wasn't home five minutes ago," Truman said. "She's not home now."

Sadie sighed and replaced the receiver on the hook. "I know."

She didn't want to sit in the dining area, where anyone passing by would be able to see them. Sadie seemed to be overly concerned about what everyone else would think. There was a very small employee break room in the back that consisted of a brown vinyl couch and a three-legged coffee table. The end without a leg was propped up with old copies of *Reader's Digest Condensed Books*, but needed at least one more to make the top of the table level. Sadie said it was a depressing little room, and Truman agreed.

Now she lowered herself to sit on the floor behind the counter, leaned her back against the shelf, and closed her eyes. "Talk to me, Truman," she said, eyes shut, ankles crossed. Yeah, she did have fine legs.

"About what?" He sat beside her, not too close, and stretched out his own legs.

She hummed as she pondered the question. "Tell me about your cabin on the lake."

Safe subject, he imagined. He wasn't much interested in safe at the moment, but Sadie obviously was.

"It's not much," he said. "A great room, two bedrooms, a big kitchen. It's the location that sold me, not the house. When I walked out onto the pier, I knew I was meant to be there."

"That's nice," she said softly. "To be somewhere and know it's your place in the world."

Sadie's place was here. Why did she fight it so hard? Why was she so damned and determined *not* to belong? "It came at a good time for me," he admitted.

She opened her eyes and stared at him, hard and soft at the same time. Only Sadie could look at a man this way, as if she could see into his soul. She was fearless and vulnerable, warm and distant. Impulsive and reserved. And he could see all that in her eyes.

"Why didn't you ever get remarried? You've been divorced, what, seven years?"

"Six."

"Plenty of time to recover, find another woman, have a couple of kids…"

Truman lifted a silencing finger. "I can't have children."

Sadie's eyes went wide and soft, her lips parted gently. "Oh. Oh, Truman, I'm so sorry."

"It's not that I *can't* have kids," he clarified, "just that it's not a good idea."

"Why not?"

He leaned slightly toward her, lowering his voice. "Kennedy married a woman who absolutely refuses to name her sons after presidents. According to my mother, I'm her last hope to carry on the McCain family tradition."

Finally, he got a real smile. A Sadie smile was enough to make a man's insides quake. "That doesn't sound so bad. I think Roosevelt and Fillmore are wonderful names."

"Oh, really." He found himself grinning back.

"And what about Nixon and McKinley?"

"McKinley McCain?"

"It has a dignified ring to it," she said, relaxing visibly.

He didn't know why he was so attracted to Sadie. Maybe because there wasn't anyone else quite like her. Not in Garth, not anywhere.

"My mother has her heart set on a grandson named Clinton."

"Bite your tongue."

"I'd rather bite yours."

Her smile faded. Maybe he should have kept his thoughts to himself, but he didn't want to play games with Sadie. He was too old to play games, and besides…time was running out. Fast. Sadie wasn't here to stay.

"So, what do you say?" he leaned toward her, moving slowly, giving her plenty of time to move away if that's really what she wanted. "Here we are with nowhere to go, nothing to do, and you disposed of the last of the lunch special, so I can't even pass the time trying to figure out what the surprise was supposed to be. And you look sexy as hell in pink."

"I don't usually wear pink," she said, her voice quick and low. "Okay, I never wear pink. It's such a girlie color. I wear black, mostly. Some navy blue. I have one dark green…"

"You're babbling."

She sighed. "I know."

Sadie's nose twitched, but she didn't turn away and she didn't tell him to back off. Just before he kissed her, she closed her eyes and parted her lips.

It started as a friendly kiss, a test and a welcome home all rolled into one. But the kiss very slowly turned into something else. Something deeper and much more compelling than a simple friendly meeting of lips. This was definitely not an ordinary kiss.

Sadie's hand came up and touched his cheek, her fingers lightly caressing, trembling and soft. That smart mouth of hers was definitely good for something besides riling him up. She knew how to kiss.

But she was still skittish. If he wasn't afraid she'd run, he'd make the next step. Deepen the kiss. Touch her the way she needed to be touched.

The tip of her tongue danced with his, and one hand settled on his arm as if it belonged there. There was electricity in the way they touched. Promise and wanting.

To hell with caution. Where was she going to run to?

Truman hauled Sadie onto his lap and wrapped his arms around her. She didn't run. She snaked her arms around his neck and tilted her head to deepen the kiss. Her body arched against his, gently, slow and soft and real. Her fingers speared through his hair and she held on to him. He felt her tremble, and he answered with one of his own.

Her indecision melted away, slowly, surely. He tasted it. Felt it. But then she took her mouth from his, laid her head on his shoulder, and sighed deeply. "We can't do this."

"We're not doing anything," Truman said, lifting his hand to thread his fingers through her dark curls. "Yet. Nothing wrong, anyway. We're both unattached and well over twenty-one, and I like you. I like you a lot, Sadie."

"Well, maybe I don't like you," she countered with very little enthusiasm.

"This is not the way to convince me that you don't like me." He raked a hand up her side and brushed his palm over her breast, over the hardened nipple beneath.

"I can't…" she began softly.

"Just a kiss, sexy Sadie, that's all I'm asking for. Just one more kiss."

She brought her mouth back to his. Just a kiss. He wanted more, he wanted everything, but not here and not while Sadie was still so damned uncertain.

Sexy Sadie. Like the song. She didn't feel sexy. At least, she hadn't until Truman had started touching her.

She had dreamed of this for years, making out with Truman McCain, wrapping her arms around his neck and playing with the little curls at the nape. Reality was so much better than fantasy. He was warm. No, hot. He was hard and soft at the same time. And he knew just how to touch and kiss and hold a woman to make her feel truly sexy.

This was not a good idea. She knew that. In just a minute, she was going to back off and tell Truman to leave her alone. In just a minute. Maybe two.

She felt as though she'd been starved for this, as though she'd been craving a kiss all her life and hadn't known it. How long had it been since a man had kissed her properly? Years. A woman shouldn't go years without a proper kiss, one that made her weak-kneed and fuzzy-headed. One that made her insides quake.

As long as she stayed in control, as long as she continued to remind herself that this attraction was physical and not emotional, she'd be all right. She concentrated on the gentle touch of Truman's mouth, his warm hands, the way her body responded. Men enjoyed physical attraction without emotion. Why couldn't she?

A firm hand raked up her side, brushed against her breast, cupped and teased. Just another minute or two, Sadie promised herself again. Maybe five.

She didn't even feel the buttons of her pink uniform come loose, but without warning Truman's hand was on the bare swell of her breasts. Fingers dancing, palm cupping. The fingers at her back twisted easily and her bra came undone. Truman's hand slipped under the loosened undergarment and touched a nipple that was so sensitive Sadie shuddered deep. She almost came, then and there.

She responded this way because it had been so long,

Sadie reasoned. A healthy woman shouldn't go for years without intimacy. Wasn't natural. She was hungry for this kind of touch, and just because it was Truman Mc-Cain who delivered it didn't mean she loved him, even a little bit. It was just…she didn't care what this was. It felt good. She liked it.

He caressed her breast with warm, gentle fingers, and a purely sexual heat shot through her. Sadie closed her eyes and just let herself feel. This was good. Beautiful and sensual and *good*. Sitting on his lap as she was, she couldn't help but notice that the kiss affected him, as well. He was hard. His erection pressed into her hip. Her fingers itched to touch his arousal, but she knew that was a move from which there was no retreat. So she un-tucked his shirt and reached beneath to touch his bare stomach, instead. He twitched and then quivered, as she settled her palm on his taut abdomen.

A big, warm hand stroked her thigh, inching higher. Truman's fingers found the thigh holster and stopped there.

He took his mouth from hers, and she looked into his eyes…but not for long. She wasn't the only one losing control. She saw too much in those blue eyes, so she closed her eyes and lowered her mouth to his neck. Heaven above, he tasted so good. Warm and male and absolutely intoxicating.

"Sadie," he whispered. "Are you on the pill or the patch or…anything?"

"No." She touched the side of his neck with the tip of her tongue. It was too late to pretend that she didn't want him with everything she had. "Do you have a condom?"

"No."

Sadie sighed and continued to kiss his neck. "Damn."

Truman laughed, low and dark. "Exactly."

It actually crossed her mind—momentarily—that one time would be safe, just once…

"I don't think I want little Clinton conceived on the floor of your Aunt Lillian's restaurant," Truman said softly.

It was a sobering statement, shocking enough to bring Sadie to her senses and make her back away from the man who held her. What had she almost done?

Nothing, Sadie assured herself silently. She'd almost done *nothing*. If Truman hadn't come to his senses, she surely would have.

She made the mistake of lifting her head to look him in the eye again. Truman had never looked at her this way before. She wanted to believe he had never looked at any woman this way before. He reached out and touched her hair. "On the other hand…"

"No," she said sharply. "You're right. Besides," she tried for a smile that didn't work. "It was just a kiss. Right?"

"Friday night," he said, his voice deep and velvety.

She was so tempted to say yes. She wanted to say yes. But if nothing else, one kiss had shown her what she already knew. Truman was a temptation that could keep her here in Garth. If she got involved with him he'd expect her to bring her life to a standstill, forget her own dreams, and stay here. For what? Sex. And in the end…after she'd given up everything for him, he'd quit looking at her this way. He'd quit kissing her like his body was on fire, he'd stop wanting her. Everything she'd sacrificed would end up being for nothing.

A man was a poor reason to change your life. She'd learned that once, and had no desire to have the lesson rammed home again.

Rammed home. Poor choice of words. Low in her gut, something quivered.

"Friday," he said again.

"No," she whispered.

The sound of a key being inserted into the lock made her jump out of her skin. If she was on the pill or if Truman had been carrying a condom in his wallet, they would be well and truly caught. Red-handed, so to speak.

"Surprise," Truman whispered.

Sadie moved off his lap and started to rise, but a strong and steady hand shot up, grabbed her wrist, and pulled her back down.

"What are you doing?" she snapped.

"Sadie…"

"Someone's coming in," she said through clenched teeth. "Someone with a key." Lillian or Mary Beth, and Sadie's money was on her aunt.

Without warning Truman kissed her quick, the grip on her wrist never wavering. "Then you'd better button your uniform," he whispered as his mouth left hers.

She glanced down at her chest, yanking her hand away from Truman as the front door swung open with a soft squeal. She buttoned furiously, watching Truman as she fastened the suddenly too-small buttons. There was still something sexy and compelling smoldering in his eyes, but a touch of humor lingered there, too.

"Wow," he mouthed as Sadie once again began to stand.

Wow, indeed.

Sadie came to her feet, heart almost steady, and came eye to eye with Aunt Lillian, over the counter.

"There you are," Lillian said with a smile. "Jennifer called me at Betty's house and said you two couldn't find the key." She shook her head. "It's right where I said it was, in the back of the knife drawer."

"You said it was under the cash register."

Aunt Lillian waved a dismissive hand. "I'm sure I said it was in the knife drawer." She was much too short to lean over the counter, but she did lean on it. "Deputy Truman, didn't I say the spare key was in the knife drawer?"

Truman sighed. "No, ma'am. You said it was under the cash register." Still, he didn't make a move to stand.

Maybe he was thinking furiously about baseball.

"Oh," Lillian said, innocent and wide-eyed. "Well, I used to keep it under the register." She shrugged her shoulders. "An easy enough mistake."

Truman finally stood. Slowly. Aunt Lillian shooed them out of the coffee shop and again locked the café door, anxious to get back to her bridge game. In the parking lot Truman waved to Lillian as she drove off, while Sadie stood there with her arms crossed over her chest.

When Aunt Lillian was gone, Truman turned his gaze back to Sadie. It made her heart—and something else—leap, but she ignored her response. "Friday night," he said again. "And this time, I'll come prepared."

Sadie shook her head. "No."

"Dinner, then back to my place."

Again, a shake of the head.

"Don't tell me you're not interested."

"I'm not interested," she said softly.

"Liar."

Sadie lifted her chin. "I did always wonder what it would be like to kiss you, but now that my curiosity has been satisfied, there's no reason to continue."

Jen crossed the parking lot, and she wasn't alone. Her friend Courtney was with her, along with two young men Sadie had not met. No wonder the rat had finally called her mother! She had plans and needed Sadie to watch the desk or clean rooms or take on some other chore the young woman didn't want.

"Hi," Jennifer said, grinning wickedly. "How did you two enjoy your afternoon?"

"Just fine," Truman answered.

"Not at all," Sadie countered. She leaned closer to her cousin and lowered her voice. "You are in so much trouble."

"Me?" Jen looked Sadie up and down, and did not bother to lower her own voice. "I'm not the one running around with my dress buttoned up crooked."

Sadie cast an uneasy glance down. Sure enough, the top button of the dreaded pink uniform had no corresponding buttonhole, and near the waist there was a telling little pooch, where there was a button-hole and no button. She felt her face turn warm. How red was she?

"I need you to cover the desk," Jennifer said. "And I cleaned some of the rooms, but didn't get to the last three yet. Thanks!"

"Be back in an hour," Sadie said sharply. "I need to get to the bank before it closes."

"An hour?" Jen whined.

"Don't be late."

Sadie watched her laughing cousin walk off with her friends. "If I kill her, will you arrest me?" she asked.

"'Fraid so," Truman said softly.

"Think a jury would convict me?"

"Probably not."

Sadie headed for the motel office. She needed a splash of cool water on her face and a change of clothes before she started cleaning those rooms.

"Sadie Mae," Truman called softly, before she'd taken half a dozen steps.

Compelled, she turned around. "I told you not to call me…"

He ignored her. "What you said yesterday, about not sleeping with me. Does that still stand?"

"'Fraid so," she said softly.

He didn't argue with her, but smiled crookedly. "Would you be really upset if I try my damnedest to make you change your mind?"

"Probably."

"I'm going to try, anyway."

No more sitting by the lake, no more kissing, no more anything! She was too close to giving in, as it was. It would be really easy to say that what was going on here was simply physical, and if they took proper precautions there was nothing at all wrong with a little adult recreational activity.

But the kiss had proven to her that, dammit, this was more than physical. For her, at least.

And that would never do.

"You could have told me I had my uniform buttoned wrong," she said, anxious to change the subject.

He grinned, darn his hide. "But it's just so cute."

"Screw you," she said as she turned her back on him again.

A sexy voice followed her. "Anytime."

Truman stuck his head in the freezer, looking for something microwaveable for dinner. He was tempted to drive to town and see if Sadie was still working the Yellow Rose Motel desk. Maybe he could talk her into a barbecue dinner at Thigpen's Pit. Then again, maybe he'd pushed enough for one day.

He ended up smiling at the ice cream, even though he didn't see anything in the freezer suitable for dinner.

Truman McCain didn't take chances, he didn't take risks, he didn't go after things he knew he shouldn't or couldn't have. Not anymore. So why the hell was he so damned and determined to get Sadie?

She was a challenge to a man who didn't want any more challenges in his life. He liked easy, he liked safe. Sadie was neither.

When a man put his hand under a woman's skirt he didn't expect to find a loaded weapon, but with Sadie Harlow anything was possible. Not an easygoing woman, she would fight him at every turn, and Truman didn't fight anymore.

The knock on his door brought his head out of the freezer. Some small hopeful part of him wondered if it was Sadie, come to finish what they'd started that afternoon, but a quick glimpse out his window proved him wrong. His mother's Caddy was parked in the front driveway.

He opened the door, and his mother lifted her head and smiled. "I brought you a casserole," she said, raising the dish high. "You never eat enough, and the recipe I tried out was just huge, and I know how you like anything spicy."

Too much explanation, too wide a smile. "Come on in," he said, opening the door and stepping back. His mother, who knew this little cabin well, walked through the great room and headed straight for the kitchen.

"Besides," she called as she walked away, "we haven't talked in ages."

"We talked yesterday," he said as he followed her into the kitchen.

"On the phone," she said, as if that explained away everything. "We haven't had a nice face-to-face talk in weeks."

She placed the covered dish on the counter and turned to grin at him.

Truman leaned against the doorway. "Okay," he said softly. "What did you hear?"

Abigail McCain, Abby to her close friends, was nearing sixty, but her short hair had been dyed a cinnamon brown. This week. He never knew what color hair his mother might have. He had accused her more than once of choosing her color blindfolded, just buying whatever box her hand happened to fall upon as she browsed through the drug store.

He didn't give her much grief, though, because changing her hair color frequently was her only real quirk. She was involved in every ladies' club in Garth, including her beloved church group. She volunteered wherever she was needed, she was always willing to lend a hand. Abby McCain missed her husband—Wilson, who'd been gone seven and a half years—but she didn't sit around and cry about the widowhood that had come to her too soon.

And her primary goal in life was to see Truman married and reproducing. He hadn't yet worked up the nerve to tell her that was never going to happen.

"Well," she said in answer to his question. "I've actually heard quite a few interesting things today."

Great. "About what?"

"About you," she said. "And that Sadie Harlow."

Uh-oh. *That* Sadie Harlow? This couldn't be good. "What did you hear?"

She pursed her lips. "I imagine you know quite well what I heard. Truman, you're a deputy. One day you'll be sheriff. You can't behave like a…a…"

"Mom…" He allowed a hit of warning to creep into his voice. He was too old for this conversation, and they both knew it.

"You don't need your name sullied by some hussy."

"Hussy?" he almost laughed.

"Truman," Abby said, lowering her voice. "She's not the right kind of girl for you. She will certainly not help with a political career."

Running for sheriff one day had been his mother's idea, and while he wasn't entirely opposed he hadn't yet embraced the concept, either.

"Sadie's not a girl, she's a woman."

Abby shook her head. "Just…behave yourself," she said primly. "You know, that nice Caroline Summers has become active in my church group. She's a teacher, you know. Elementary school. All those children just love her. One day she'll make some man a fine wife, and don't you just know she'll be a wonderful mother?" Her smile bloomed. "We're having a get-together at the house Friday night to finalize the plans for our booth at the Big

Bass Festival. You should stop by." She actually managed to sound as if it were a spur-of-the-moment idea.

"I have plans for Friday night."

Her smile died quickly. "With that Sadie Harlow?"

"Yes, with that Sadie Harlow."

She shook a finger in his direction. "You've forgotten, but when she was a teenager she was in all kinds of trouble."

"Sadie?"

"She smoked. And many was the night I got a phone call from her aunt, wondering where she was." She nodded her head knowingly. "I believe they caught her drinking once."

He loved his mother, he truly did, but she did not know when to quit.

"I don't think she smokes anymore," he said. "I haven't seen her light up, anyway." And she didn't smell or taste like cigarette smoke. He didn't point this out to his mother. "She still stays out late, though," he added with a smile.

"So I hear."

"Don't know if she drinks or not, but thanks for the suggestion." He winked at his mother, who turned a little pink in the face. "Next time we go out to Miranda Lake I'll take along a bottle and get Sadie good and liquored up."

She shook that finger again. "You're too much like your father."

"Did he drive you out to Miranda Lake and get you liquored up?"

She turned around and grabbed her casserole dish. "No. Of course not! But he never took anything seriously either, especially when I had a legitimate concern."

Chin high, mouth pursed, she headed for Truman and the door, casserole in hand.

"Sorry," he said, stepping aside so she could pass. "I didn't mean to make you mad." He followed her into the great room.

"Of course you did," she said. "You knew exactly what you were doing. You always do." She turned and sighed. "Caroline Summers is so sweet."

Caroline Summers was sleeping with George Baker, the school principal. They tried to be discreet, so only half the town knew about the affair. George was almost twenty years older than Caroline, and was in the midst of a nasty divorce.

Besides, Caroline Summers didn't turn his crank the way Sadie did.

"Yes, she's very sweet," he agreed. "If it makes you feel any better, Sadie doesn't want to have anything to do with me."

"That's not the way I heard it." Abby stopped and turned slowly. "You said the two of you had a date Friday night."

"We do. Sadie just hasn't agreed yet."

Her eyes softened. Maybe her chin trembled, just a little. "I don't want to see you hurt."

Again. She didn't say that, but then, she didn't have to. That *again* lurked in her worried eyes.

"I'll be fine."

She handed over the casserole dish, and Truman took it. "There's not any gelatin in here, is there?" he asked suspiciously.

"Of course not!"

"Good."

Chapter 5

Sadie did not wear pink for her late afternoon visit to the bank, and in the name of sheer good sense she left her pistol locked in the glove box of her Toyota. She wore a black skirt, short but not too short, and a black blouse that was cut low enough to advertise her figure but not low enough to be called slutty. Neither was two sizes too large. Her heels were high, but not too high. Her makeup was tasteful, though the lipstick was a little bit too red to be considered boring. She wanted to look professional when she interviewed Rhea whatever. It would be tricky, getting information out of Aidan Hearn's secretary without pushing or allowing the woman to figure out that Sadie had no business investigating her deceased boss's murder.

Garth's First National Bank was a small but stately building, one of those old edifices the historical societies always loved so much. Brick, square and massive, it was a testament to wealth and power and the Old South.

Sadie walked into the building, doing her best to act as if she belonged. On her first visit she'd had to ask directions. Today she knew just where she was going.

Rhea sat at her desk as she had on Monday afternoon, displaying her grief by lazily shaping her nails with an emery board. There was a name plate on her desk. Rhea Powell.

Rhea was blond, her boobs were surely not natural and she wore too much makeup for a woman of her age. She was not much older than Sadie and might even be a couple of years younger, but the way she had the makeup caked on she appeared to be an older woman who looked good for her age.

She was definitely proud of the boobs. The white blouse she wore plunged deeply into cleavage territory.

Rhea dropped her emery board and pointed at Sadie. "You're a day early, and besides, Mr. Hearn is dead."

"I know."

"I know you know," Rhea said sharply. "You found him, and after that scene you made in the office Monday afternoon, I'm afraid I just had to tell the cops that you might've killed him in a rage or something."

It would be so easy to argue with the woman. There would be no contest, not in a battle of the wits or a physical confrontation. But shouting Rhea down wouldn't get Sadie anywhere.

Sadie let her lower lip tremble slightly, as if she were upset. "I'm sorry. Has someone else taken over Mr. Hearn's accounts? I really must talk to a bank officer about my problem."

"Mr. Elliot has taken over, but he's really not up to speed and this is a very busy day, so an appointment today is simply out of the question."

Busy my ass. Sadie contained her impulsive response, and bit her lower lip. "I understand."

Rhea lifted her eyebrows slightly, surprised by Sadie's calm reaction.

"I really should apologize for my behavior Monday afternoon," Sadie stepped closer to the desk, her eyes scanning as quickly and meekly as possible. Emery board, nail polish, small mirror, one thin file—name not readable from this vantage point. Sadie leaned slightly over the desk and whispered, "PMS."

Rhea waved a limp-wristed hand. "I totally understand."

"The murder must be a real shocker for you. I mean, you worked with Mr. Hearn, so it must be hard to imagine him…you know, dead like that."

"Yeah," Rhea answered. "I haven't gotten a whole lot of sleep this week, you know."

The secretary looked perfectly well-rested, but Sadie didn't think it would be wise to point that out. "What kind of a boss was he?"

Rhea shrugged. "Pretty good, I guess. He didn't mind when I took a long lunch, and he always gave me a really good Christmas bonus."

"How long did you work for him?"

"Almost five years."

Sadie nodded as if she were very interested. "Are you going to stay on with Mr. Elliot?"

"I don't know yet," Rhea said. "He hasn't really decided. But I can make an appointment for you." She grabbed an appointment book from her drawer and flipped through to Monday morning. "How about ten?"

"There's nothing tomorrow, or maybe Friday?"

"No. Mr. Elliot is really slammed for tomorrow, and he works a half day on Friday. And he's still trying to acquaint himself with the new job and all."

"I can imagine." Sadie propped her hip on the desk. "Did Mr. Hearn work any half days?"

Rhea laughed as she wrote Sadie's name on the line that read 10:00 a.m. "Lots. That's another reason he was such a good boss." She glanced up. "He wasn't here all that much. He said he got more business done playing eighteen holes of golf than he could in his office."

"Wow," Sadie said softly. "That does make for a good job, I guess, when the boss is gone half the time."

Rhea's smile turned smug. "Better than slinging grits, that's for sure."

Sadie didn't lash out as she wanted to. Her smile actually widened. "Sounds like you had it made here. Short hours, not much actual work to do. So, were you sleeping with Mr. Hearn?"

A hand that was in the process of being manicured reacted with a jerk that sent a bottle of nail polish spinning, and the pupils of Rhea's eyes darkened. "I think you'd better leave now." Her voice trembled as she retrieved the nail polish.

Damn. It had been a shot in the dark, a potshot to counter the comment about slinging grits. But Rhea's reaction had been more than one of outrage. She hadn't been insulted, she was scared.

Sadie had her other woman. One of them, at least.

* * *

Sadie had managed to weasel out of breakfast duty today, thank goodness. Truman had eaten his breakfast at the café. From her bedroom window, she'd seen his patrol car drive up. She'd watched him walk to the door, watched as the heavy glass door slowly closed behind him.

No, she couldn't stand there and pour coffee and smile at Truman as if nothing had changed. Everyone had surely heard what had happened yesterday—the early morning arrival after spending the night in his truck and/or the incident in the café.

Sadie spent the late-morning hours helping her aunt pay bills and balance the books. Jimmy Harlow had always handled the finances, and even now, four years after his death, his widow had to be guided through the process. It wasn't that Lillian wasn't capable of doing the books; she simply didn't want to. It was something Sadie could do, besides cleaning nasty rooms and slinging grits, and she found making the numbers add up oddly soothing. Right now she needed a little order in a world gone wacko.

While she was here, she really needed to get Aunt Lillian a program so they could do the financial work on the computer. These paper records were archaic.

She went over the numbers there at the front desk, ready to take any calls that came in, glad it had been a slow morning. It was almost noon. Jennifer was still in bed, and with the books mostly done, Lillian had returned to her station at the café, where the lunch crowd needed her.

Her aunt wouldn't admit that anything was wrong,

but Sadie could tell Lillian had been shaken by the discovery of a body in one of her motel rooms. True, Aidan Hearn had not been one of her favorite people, but still…she'd known him. At least she hadn't been forced to see the body. Sadie had never met Hearn, and finding the body was an unpleasant experience *she* had no desire to repeat. Yeah, it was definitely better that she'd been the one to find the body. It would have been tough on Lillian, and if Jennifer had been the one to stumble into that bathroom she'd probably still be screaming.

The quiet was nice. Sadie was able to calmly plan her revenge uninterrupted. Her cousin would pay, one way or another. For calling the sheriff because Sadie had been out late, for leaving Sadie and Truman locked in the café, for always foisting off the more unpleasant chores to her cousin…

When the lobby door swung open, Sadie lifted her head from the books, hoping 104 was checking out today. If she had to empty one more trash can full of dirty diapers, scrape up one more scattered fast-food dinner…

But it wasn't 104. It was Truman, wearing his uniform since today was obviously a work day. She took a moment to admire the way he looked, tall and well-built in that uniform that looked as if it had been made to fit him, before taking a deep breath and preparing herself to send him on his way. As quickly as possible.

"Lost?" she asked briskly.

"Nope," he answered as he walked toward the desk.

"Are you here to arrest me?"

He shook his head. "Lunch break."

She lifted a hand and pointed out the window.

"Wrong building, Einstein. The café's on the other side of the parking lot."

"It's pretty full right now. Thursday is Chicken Fried Steak. I thought I'd wait until the crowd died down." He leaned against the desk. "So, why aren't you working today?"

"I am working."

"In the café," he clarified.

"Mary Beth's working an extra shift today, and Aunt Lillian and Bowie are there. They don't need me, thank goodness." She lifted one hand to shoo him silently away, turning her attention to the books before her.

He did turn and walk away, to the coffeepot near the end of the desk. He poured a cup—what was left in the carafe. It had been sitting there a while.

Truman took a sip and then turned to her. "Sadie, did you make this coffee?"

"Yes, I did," she said with a smile.

"It's awful."

"Maybe you should get your caffeine needs met elsewhere."

He took another sip. "Nah. It's already growing on me." He sat in the padded chair near the window, foam coffee cup in hand. "This coffee has character."

He was flirting with her. Smiling, flooding the room with testosterone. Making her feel, with his very presence, on edge and itchy and quivery.

Sadie slapped down her pencil. "Truman McCain, what's it going to take to get rid of you?"

He smiled. "More than bad coffee and that sad attempt at a steely glare."

Sad attempt? Sadie knew without doubt that her steely glare worked wonders when it came to scaring off men. She was still giving Truman that look when the phone rang. Thank God.

"Yellow Rose Motel," she answered crisply.

"Sadie?" She couldn't quite place the voice. It was deep, sexy, very warm and nicely Southern.

"Yes?"

"Jason Davenport."

She looked at Truman and grinned. "Jason Davenport!" she said. "Why, what a nice surprise."

"I heard you were back in town, and I just had to call and say hello."

She pictured him in her mind. Tall, broad-shouldered, black-haired and green-eyed. Jason had been pretty as all get out, especially as he'd tried to sweet-talk her out of her virginity. He'd disappeared quickly once she'd said no, so she really should hang up on him and be done with it.

But Truman was listening. "Well, it's really great to hear your voice."

Jason cleared his throat, hummed and hawed a little. "I had been thinking maybe I'd ask you out for dinner or something, but I heard you were seeing Truman McCain."

"Where did you hear that?" She leaned against the counter, catching just a glimpse of Truman out of the corner of her eye. He looked the other way, but he listened intently. "I'm not seeing anyone," she added.

"Oh, yeah?" Jason said brightly. "That's great. I thought I was a day late and a dollar short. You know, I used to like Truman, but not today. The bastard gave me a speeding ticket this morning. I wasn't going more than five miles an hour over the speed limit, and he pulled me over and wrote me up right there. Wouldn't just give me a warning."

"That doesn't sound right," she said, commiserating sweetly. "How *rude*."

"Yeah. That is rude." Jason cleared his throat. "Anyway, if you're not seeing him, maybe we can get together. Tomorrow night?"

Sadie sighed. Well, this was a fine mess. Jason was handsome and had a great voice, but he'd tried to sleep with her and then dumped her thirteen years ago. What kind of self-respecting woman would go out with him again?

But she couldn't refuse. Not in front of Truman. If she agreed to go out with Jason when she continually refused to accept Truman's invitation, maybe he'd be pissed enough to leave her alone.

"I'd love to get together tomorrow night." Sadie smiled. She'd be seen with Jason, people would quit talking about her and Truman, and Truman would finally get the idea that she was not interested. Then she'd end the date early. She was too old to fall for Jason's slick ways. "I hear you're some kind of artist?"

Truman calmly took a sip of his coffee. He picked up a leaflet from the table at his side. The brochure was all about the Big Bass Festival. He read it carefully, as if he didn't already know every detail.

"Yeah," Jason answered. "Maybe tomorrow night I can show you some of my work."

"That would be great."

"I'll pick you up at eight."

She remembered Tuesday night and the too-late realization that she should've taken her own car to meet

Truman for dinner. "I can meet you somewhere. There's no reason for you to go out of your way to pick me up."

"No, I insist," Jason said. "I have to drive right by the motel, anyway."

"But…"

"I insist," Jason said again.

Truman was listening closely, even though he tried to look like he couldn't hear a word that was said. Ha. "Well, if you're coming this way anyway… Eight it is."

They said goodbye, and Sadie sighed as she hung up the phone. "It seems I have a date for tomorrow night," she said, keeping her eyes on the books that were spread across the front counter. "Jason Davenport."

"I thought you were busy," Truman said nonchalantly as he perused the brochure.

"Change of plans."

Truman returned the pamphlet to the table, tossed his almost-empty foam cup in the trash, and stood slowly. "Well, have fun. I'm going to grab some lunch." As he pushed open the door, he flashed her a too-charming grin.

So much for breaking Truman's heart.

It wasn't fifteen minutes later that a young girl carrying a bulky knapsack walked through that same door, her eyes flitting this way and that.

"Can I help you?"

The girl was skittish. Not quite scared, but not exactly strong, either. One good "boo" would probably send her back out the door again. She didn't look to be much older than Jennifer, and her long pale-brown hair had been pulled back into a loose ponytail. She was pretty enough, but wore no makeup. Her clothes were at least a size too big, baggy and nondescript.

"Can I help you?" Sadie asked again.

The girl looked Sadie in the eye. Maybe she wasn't wimpy after all. Just cautious. There was something vaguely familiar about her, too, as if they'd met once, long ago.

"I'm looking for a job," the girl said softly.

"Ever worked in a motel or a restaurant before?"

"Both."

Sadie glanced heavenward and mouthed, "Thank you."

"I need a place to stay, too," the girl said quickly. "I'm new in town, and I don't have much cash with me."

"Room and board come with the job," Sadie said. She'd just made that decision. "Can you start today? Now?"

Wide-eyed, the girl nodded.

Sadie smiled. "Great. What's your name?"

"Kathy Carson."

"I have a horrendous pink uniform upstairs with my name on it. It's yours. We'll take care of the paperwork later."

The girl nodded and looked at Sadie with the saddest, greenest eyes. "Later is good for me."

Sadie smiled at the timid girl. Kathy had the wary look of a woman who was hiding from something. Or someone. Sadie had become accustomed to seeing that look over the years. This could be the perfect job for Kathy.

Garth was a great place to hide.

It was late in the afternoon when Sadie finally caught up with her cousin. Jennifer had slept late, and then hit the occupied rooms for cleaning. She'd managed to stay out of Sadie's way all day, and had even taken care of

104. She knew she was in big trouble, otherwise she would have run to Sadie for help.

When they'd been growing up, Jennifer, the baby, had been strictly hands off. After all, she was just a kid, and Sadie had been told countless times that she was supposed to know better.

They were both over twenty-one, now, and all bets were off.

Sadie stepped into the room where Jennifer sat at her vanity, carefully applying her makeup. She closed the door behind her. "More plans for the evening?" she asked softly.

Jen didn't take her eyes off her own face in the mirror. "Just dinner with friends. Porter Manly is going to fill in for Conrad, since he still hasn't shown up."

Sadie leaned against the closed door. "We haven't had a chance to talk about yesterday."

Jennifer's smile was wide and wicked. "Man, it was wild. We laughed about that all night. You two came out of the café looking like you'd just finished doing it right there on the counter."

Sadie had been mad enough when she'd walked into the room, but that *we laughed all night* hit a tender cord, and her heartbeat and her anger revved up a bit.

"Nothing happened."

"Yeah, right," Jennifer said, returning her attention to her reflection.

"All you had to do was call Lillian and get her over here with the key," Sadie said, almost calm. "One phone call."

"Why didn't you call her yourself?"

"I didn't know where she was. You did."

"I don't hear Truman complaining," Jennifer teased.

Sadie took a deep, calming breath. "I'm going to get

you, Jen. I don't know how, or when, but I'm going to make it my mission in life to embarrass you the way you embarrassed me."

"I didn't unbutton your uniform," Jennifer argued, her grin staying in place. "And I didn't button it up crooked, either. It's not my fault you were embarrassed. You must've been in quite a hurry when you buttoned up." She put her mascara down. "Besides, I don't embarrass the way you do. Who sucked all the fun out of you, anyway? The guy you were supposed to get married to? That was years ago…"

"Leave Spencer out of this," Sadie said softly.

Jennifer spun around and looked Sadie up and down. "I don't know what you're so riled up about. Truman has the hots for you, you have the hots for him. All I did was nudge things along a bit."

"I do not have the hots for Truman!"

"Of course you do. You have for years. Everyone knows it."

Everyone knows it. Her worst nightmare. "I'll have you know, I have a date tomorrow night, and it's not with Truman."

"Oh, yeah? With who, then?"

If Jennifer knew who Sadie was going out with, she'd probably track Jason down and do something devious to ruin the evening. She'd set something up, of that Sadie had no doubt. "None of your business."

Jennifer waved a dismissive hand. "Okay, so I was wrong. If you don't want Truman, maybe I'll go after him myself." She arched her back, checking out young breasts that were molded in a snug blue sweater.

Sadie's heart lurched. When it came to attracting

men, she didn't hold a candle to her little cousin. She knew it, and so did Jennifer. "Fine," she said calmly.

"Fine?" Jennifer fluffed her blond hair. "You know, I could have had Truman ages ago, but he never seemed, I don't know, very exciting. But the way he looked at you yesterday when y'all walked out of the coffee shop, like he wanted to toss you up on the hood of his patrol car and nail you then and there...it was definitely very sexy."

"He did not look like..."

"He did," Jen said confidently.

"I can't speak for anyone else, but I certainly don't have the hots for any man in Garth. If you want Truman, please be my guest."

"Sadie," Jen said sharply, "you can tell me you don't want Truman all you want, you can even stand there and give me permission to have at him myself. But you can't convince me that he doesn't want you." She shrugged her shoulders. "Doesn't matter. Guys don't moon after women who don't want them. Not for long, anyway. They aren't built that way. Sooner or later, probably sooner, Truman will get tired of butting his head against a stone wall. Maybe when he starts looking around for a woman who's more agreeable than you are, I'll be there."

Sadie shook her head. "There's something wrong with you."

"You think so?"

Something Sadie didn't care to examine hurt. A sharp pang shot through her chest. Something low in her body rumbled. She recognized the reaction for what it was. Fear.

"Truman has been right under your nose for years,

and you don't find him attractive until you think I do. That's sick."

"So you *do* want him."

"I didn't say that."

Jennifer rolled her eyes as she stood. "You know what your problem is, Sadie?"

"No, but I feel quite certain you're going to tell me."

"You think too much." Jennifer grabbed her purse off the bed and walked toward the door Sadie blocked.

"That's not a criticism I'm going to take seriously, coming from a woman who doesn't think at all," Sadie countered.

"I think," Jennifer said, apparently not at all insulted. "But I also feel. These days you dissect every little thing until it doesn't have any heart left." She stopped before Sadie and posed, arms crossed, chin lifted. "Okay," she said in a lowered voice. "Maybe I don't have the hots for Truman, maybe I don't want to be there to cushion the blow when he realizes you really don't want to have anything to do with him. But he's a nice guy, and I do like him." She shook her head. "I just don't want you to dissect the heart out of him. He deserves better than that."

Sadie stepped aside and let her cousin open the door. She'd come to her cousin's room thinking of revenge, and instead of feeling righteous and justified, she felt chastened and deflated.

"Truman knows exactly how I feel."

"Please," Jennifer scoffed as she headed for the stairs. "*You* don't know how you feel."

Sadie hadn't had anyone to really talk to in so long, she'd forgotten what it was like. She worked with guys who didn't exactly go around talking about their feel-

ings. She trusted them to watch her back, and they
trusted her. But she didn't know if Lucky was Santana's
real name or a nickname, or if Dante had ever been
married, or if Murphy had a serious side. Cal never
talked about whether or not he and his new wife planned
to have children any time soon, or even how Livvie
liked the new house.

She'd been living with superficial conversations instead of heartfelt confessions. Here she was, marking
time, just waiting for her chance to get out of Garth all
over again. And there was no one she could talk to.

God, she sounded like such a *girl*.

"I'm not going to be here very long," she said to Jennifer's back. "It wouldn't make any sense for me to get
involved with Truman or anyone else, no matter how I
feel." Her heart thudded. "No sense at all."

At the top of the stairs, Jennifer stopped and spun
around to face Sadie. "Want a little advice?"

"From you?" Sadie tried to sound sufficiently cold,
but a small tremor in her voice gave her away.

"Have some fun, for once in your life. Have a fling
with Truman, if that's what you both want." For a split
second, Jen looked more like a woman than a spoiled
little girl. "Don't dissect it. Don't analyze it. Don't
worry about what's going to happen tomorrow or next
week or next year. Just cut loose and let your life un-
fold, instead of trying so damn hard to plan every detail. Sadie, you're working so hard at looking ahead
that you're missing right now. All we have is right now."

With that, Jennifer bounded down the stairs.

Sadie sagged against the wall. When Jennifer started
making sense, the world really had gone mad.

Chapter 6

Sadie chewed on whether or not she should tell Evans that she suspected Rhea Powell had been sleeping with Hearn. She finally decided against it. She had no proof, other than a woman's intuition. If Evans was smart he'd find out on his own. Rhea wasn't a very good liar. She'd probably give herself away, sooner rather than later. Any attempt by Sadie to get more involved than she should be would only set off Evans' radar. Best to lay low, for now.

Sadie didn't work murder cases; that wasn't her job. She had searched for and found missing children, rescued kidnapped kids like Danny, and even tailed terrorists, on one occasion. Now and then they were hired to retrieve things, not people, but the jobs remained much the same. Along with other Benning agents she'd been to Mexico and other points south, as well as an island in the Caribbean. There had been that one really wild trip to Europe.

She was involved in the action, not investigation. But that didn't mean she couldn't think.

People didn't get killed for no reason. Well, with the exception of the occasional victim of a serial killer, of course, but in this instance that was an unlikely scenario. Drugs, love, sex, money. That's why people got murdered. Had Hearn been involved with drugs? Not that she'd been able to uncover, but that didn't mean anything. Love? She almost snorted. Men like Hearn didn't love anyone but themselves. Sex. Obviously he'd been fooling around on poor Mrs. Hearn. Had he been cheating on Rhea as well? Too soon to know.

Money. Hearn had been knee-deep in money, his own and the bank's. Who knows what else he might've been knee-deep in?

Sadie had tried to see Hearn's widow yesterday afternoon, between Truman's visit to her and her talk with Jennifer, but the woman had been in seclusion. Mourning or celebrating? It was impossible to know. All Lillian would say about Evelyn Hearn was the woman was very sweet. That "very sweet" was followed by a pursing of the lips, as if Lillian was physically stopping more information from coming out of her mouth. After a while Sadie stopped pressing.

She was beginning to get worried about Conrad. He still hadn't shown up, and while he had always been undependable, she didn't think it was like him to be gone for three full days without anyone being able to find him. There was no apparent connection between Hearn and Conrad Hudson, and in truth they had never run in the same social circles.

Worst case, the killer knew Conrad had seen him or her, and the Yellow Rose Motel's part-time night-desk clerk was dead, too.

At least the employee situation was under control. Kathy wasn't only experienced, she was good. That morning there had been no spilled coffee, and she'd very quickly learned to banter with the customers. Lillian loved her. Sadie loved her, primarily because with Kathy on the payroll she didn't have to worry about serving Truman coffee or grits or anything else.

Porter Manley had agreed to take on the night-shift position full time, at least for now. Sadie didn't get the same warm, fuzzy feeling from Manley that she got from Kathy. Not that there was anything outright wrong with him. He showed up for work clean, he kept the office neat, and when he made himself something to eat he always cleaned up his own mess.

But he never said much. Porter was one of those silent types who kept to himself.

It was Friday morning and Sadie's turn to watch the front desk. So when Kathy stopped by the office to grab a cup of coffee before beginning to clean the occupied rooms, Sadie was glad of the chance to talk.

"Sorry you walked through that door, yet?" Sadie asked with a smile.

Kathy returned the smile, almost reluctantly. "No. I don't mind working hard. I'd just as soon stay busy."

"I am going to hire someone else," Sadie promised. "Things will settle down around here, soon enough."

The girl sipped at her coffee, then nodded agreeably.

It was a tough life to live on the run. Who was Kathy hiding from? Husband, boyfriend, father? Sadie had to give Kathy credit for taking her life into her own hands. She hadn't been one to sit at home and take whatever the man she was running from dished out. There was some pride in that decision; and more than a little strength. Kathy, timid as she appeared to be, was a survivor. Still, it was a hard life for one so young.

Sadie leaned on the front desk. "You and Jennifer must be about the same age." Close enough, anyway. "When you have some free time, maybe she can show you around town. Granted, there's not much to show."

Kathy shook her head. "I don't go out."

It made Sadie angry to think of what someone must've done to Kathy to make her live this way.

"I can show you a few moves if you like," she said. "Nothing fancy, but every woman needs to be able to defend herself."

Kathy's head snapped up, and she was outwardly alarmed.

Yeah, some man had done his best to ruin her. "A little karate, some plain old street tricks…"

"No thanks," Kathy said quickly. "I, uh, I get along okay. The coffee was good," she added quickly, "but I need to get to work."

Head down, the new girl did just that. She slipped out the door and headed for the small room where the cleaning supplies were stored.

It was a shame that Kathy had allowed one bad apple to ruin her life. A woman shouldn't let a single bad experience, no matter how bad, stop her from living.

With a small jolt, Sadie realized that what she'd done

wasn't all that different. Spencer had been her bad apple, and while he had never hit her, she'd allowed him to bring her life—part of it, at least—to a halt.

Until she'd come back to Garth, she'd hadn't even missed that part of her life. Now, she felt a little sad and empty.

Some things couldn't be fixed with a swift kick or a bullet.

The sheriff would call this "highly irregular." The ABI agent, Evans, would probably call it "illegal."

Of course, Truman hadn't gone looking for Hearn's widow, and that made all the difference. He and Evelyn Hearn just happened to be waiting in line at the grocery store, him with his coffee and frozen dinners, her with her diet soda and cookies.

She'd looked back and up at him and he'd nodded. He'd offered his sympathies and she'd teared up. It was neighborly kindness, not investigative skills, that found Truman and a sniffling Evelyn Hearn sitting together at a small table in Thigpen's Pit, sipping coffee and talking about her late husband.

"He wasn't a good husband," Mrs. Hearn said between sniffles. "Oh, he provided a nice home and I always had all the jewelry and clothes I wanted, and the kids got a good college education, but…" she shook her head, and graying hair danced around her drawn face. "He wasn't a good husband," she said again, more softly this time.

"I understand," Truman said.

"Do you?" The older woman looked him squarely in the eye. "A man like you, I bet you have no idea what it's like to dearly and completely love someone who doesn't love you back."

"Now, why would you think that?"

She fluttered a dismissive hand. "You're a man. Men don't suffer in the same way women do, when it comes to matters of the heart."

"I believe you're mistaken." His own heart had taken a bit of a beating, and had taken a while to recover. But apparently it had recovered. He was having all sorts of unexpected thoughts about Sadie these days.

Finally, Evelyn Hearn sighed. "Are you going to find the man who did this to my Aidan?"

He wasn't a part of the investigative team, but that detail didn't matter to Evelyn Hearn at the moment. "Yes ma'am."

"Good. Aidan was a liar and a cheat, a bad husband and an indifferent father. But he was all I had and I want whoever took him from me to pay."

"I understand the funeral is going to take place Monday."

"Yes. I would have liked to have it sooner, but…" her eyes watered up again. "They insisted that an autopsy was necessary, and they've sent Aidan's body to Montgomery. That's just not right, is it? I hate the thought of his body being poked and prodded and…" She shuddered. "I can't think about what they're doing to him down there. But the investigator from the ABI, he promised me that Aidan would be released by this weekend, Sunday at the latest, and we can have a proper burial on Monday."

In his mind, Truman struck Evelyn Hearn from his own list of suspects. She was devastated. Angry, yes. Betrayed, without a doubt. But she'd loved her husband.

"Tell me about him," Truman prodded gently. He didn't know if he'd learn anything of interest about Garth's murder victim, but it couldn't hurt to ask.

Jason would be here at eight. Sadie spent a little extra time making herself pretty for the date. Since she'd slept in her little black dress on Tuesday night and hadn't yet carried it to the cleaners, she wasn't wearing it again. Besides, she had been overdressed for her dinner with Truman. Since Bob's Steak and Fixin's was the nicest place in town, she imagined that's where Jason would take her.

So tonight she wore crisp black slacks, low-cut leather boots with a neat and unobtrusive holster for her pistol, and a lightweight cream sweater that molded to her curves. Even though the outfit was more casual than what she'd worn for her dinner with Truman, it was still very nice and more than a little sexy. If they happened to run into Truman while they were out, she wouldn't want him to think that she'd put any less effort into this date than she had for theirs. Not that Tuesday's dinner had been a date.

There it was again—the girlie-girl in her rising to the surface. Yeah, she had to get out of Garth. The sooner the better.

Porter Manly was on the desk again tonight, and Lillian had gone to bed early. This whole business with Hearn had poor Lillian exhausted. Kathy was settled into Room 102, and Jennifer had left almost two hours ago. She never said where she was going. Just "out."

At eight on the nose, a car pulled into the parking lot. Sadie waited in the lobby, not exactly anxious to see Jason again but curious to discover if anything about him kindled the same intense feelings Truman roused. Maybe her reaction to Truman was just hormones running out of control. A little wacky chemistry, since thirty was coming and she hadn't settled down into the domestic life most women were supposed to crave on some primal level. Yea, that was it. Hormones. If she remembered correctly, Jason Davenport had managed to stir her teenage hormones very nicely.

The vehicle that parked near the door had seen better days, and it was quite small. The compact car sported one fender that was a different color than the rest of the vehicle. It looked very much like a clown car.

Just as with a proper clown car, the man who climbed out of the driver's side was a big guy, and his clothes were a size too small. Pants too tight, buttons of the shirt strained to the limit, it was almost painful to watch him move in those tight clothes. The hair that hung to his shoulders didn't hide the fact that his hairline was receding. He carried a crumpled paper bag.

Oh God, were those sideburns? They were huge. Elvis-style.

The big guy with the sideburns opened the door and stepped into the lobby, but instead of walking to the desk he turned to her and smiled.

And Sadie's heart leapt into her throat. "Jason…. Hi."

"Zowee, Sadie." He looked her up and down without an ounce of finesse. "You look hot."

"Thanks." The word came out much too small.

"Really hot," he said again, with emphasis.

This time Sadie's thanks were lost in her throat.

"I brought you something." He handed over the bag. "As you know, I'm somewhat of a local artist."

"That's what I hear." She grasped the paper bag tightly.

"Go on," he said, nodding to the crumpled brown bag and gesturing with one chunky hand. "Open it."

Sadie turned her attention to the bag. No wonder Truman had smiled when he'd learned that she was going out with Jason tonight! No wonder he wasn't worried about her date with the local artist. The high-school heartthrob had turned into a joke, with the extra weight around the middle and the outrageous sideburns and the clown car.

She reached into the bag and pulled out his artwork, and added *wooden fish* to the running list of the absurd. She supposed it was wood sculpture. The fish—a large-mouth bass if she wasn't mistaken—was painted turquoise and bright yellow and pink. It was hideous.

"Wow," she muttered, unable to come up with anything else.

"I sell these pieces at the Festival for thirty-nine bucks, but for you...I'll only charge an even fifteen." He grinned widely.

He expected her to *pay* for this? *Money?* She tried to return the fish. "I don't have the right change with me."

He held up his hands, palms front. "No, no. I won't make you give it back now that you've seen it. You can owe me."

"Gee." Her heart sank to her stomach. "Thanks."

Jason Davenport had been beautiful in high school, a talented football player with a great smile and a bucketful of charm. Now that she thought about it, she remembered that he had never been known for his brains.

With the fish tucked in the crook of her arm, in the hopes that at sometime during the evening she could manage to return it without being hopelessly cruel, Sadie followed Jason to his jalopy. She wasn't a demanding woman, not at all. She wasn't a snob. But the idea of being seen with Jason in this car was downright humiliating.

Sadie held her head high as she moved aside a barbecue wrapper from the passenger seat, before sitting. She'd done this to herself, and there was no backing out now. She'd made her bed and…

No, she wasn't even going to think about *bed*. She and Jason would catch up on what had been happening to them in the past ten years or so, they'd have a nice dinner and some light conversation, and if he tried anything…

Well, she was armed.

Truman had suspected the Shamrock was the kind of place Jason Davenport would take a date. Located on the edge of town, it was cheap, loud and crude. He'd been right. Just after eight-fifteen, Jason and Sadie arrived.

It probably took a lot these days to shake or surprise Sadie Harlow. She wasn't visibly horrified or disappointed by the roadhouse where the crasser element in the county hung out on the weekend.

But it was clear to anyone with two eyes that she didn't belong here. Sadie was a pearl in a bowl of grits, polished and beautiful. No matter how she tried to look as though she fit in here…she never would. Never.

Sitting at the bar, Truman turned his face away from the door and took a long swig of the beer he'd been nursing. The place was crowded tonight, and if he was careful Sadie would never know he was here. Jason led her to a table in the far corner, stopping along the way to say hello to several friends. Apparently this was a regular stop for Davenport.

It had happened a long time ago, and goodness knows none of them were the same people they had been as teenagers. He'd made mistakes in those days and so had Sadie. So did everyone. At the old age of thirty-three Truman couldn't even remember how his brain had functioned at sixteen and seventeen; he couldn't reconstruct in his mind his reasoning for some of the things he'd done. And still, he couldn't forgive Jason for using Sadie and then dropping her. She deserved better, then and now.

The crowded dance floor spread between the bar and the table where Jason and Sadie sat, and so did a number of patrons who stood and visited rather than dancing or sitting. Sadie would have to look in just the right place at just the right moment in order to see him sitting here. He could keep an eye on her, make sure the evening went smoothly, and she'd never realize he was watching.

He should've known better. Sadie and her date for the evening hadn't been at the Shamrock for ten minutes before he glanced toward the table and found her staring at him. No smile, no nod. Just a stare. Even though the space between them was broken often by enthusiastic dancers passing by, she looked directly at him. And then she returned her attention to her date, and Truman had the distinct feeling that he'd just been dismissed.

Women.

"Dinner" was hot wings and celery sticks and beer. Sadie ate the wings without complaint, polished off all the celery sticks, and sipped on the beer. She could hold her liquor just fine, thank you, but she did not intend to be in the least impaired tonight.

While Jason went on and on about his career as an "artist," leaning over the table and all but shouting to be heard over the jukebox that blared country-and-western music at a deafening level, Sadie nodded as if she were paying attention and let her mind wander.

Was it a coincidence that Truman was drinking here tonight? Unlikely. He'd come here to gloat, maybe to have himself a laugh at her expense. This had to be amusing for him. He was such a rat for not warning her about Jason, she didn't think she could ever forgive him.

Of course, she had blatantly used Jason in order to sting Truman's pride, so that probably wasn't fair.

She almost hoped there was a ruckus tonight, so she could blow off a little steam. This was definitely the sort of place where ruckuses happened with regularity, so she held on to that hope as Jason rambled on. Some unpleasant man would make an unwelcome pass and she'd knock him flat on his back with a single move. The place was lousy with unpleasant men and a few of them had actually leered at her, so that scenario wasn't out of the realm of possibility. A bar fight might break out, and instead of squealing to be protected, she'd jump right in and hold her own. Wouldn't that give them all something to talk about?

While Jason talked about his last exciting trip to a well-respected Birmingham flea market to sell wooden fish painted in garish colors—her description of his "art," not his—she glanced toward the bar. Truman was still there, sitting all alone and nursing the same damn beer that had been in front of him when she and Jason had arrived. On occasion, one woman or another would sit at the stool beside him and try to strike up a conversation, but those women never lasted long. Sadie wished she was sitting closer so she could read their lips. A single man who looked like Truman sitting at the bar wouldn't stay single long. Unless he wanted it that way.

Like it or not, she'd give her right arm to be sitting beside Truman instead of sitting here.

Jason leaned over the table, as much as his beer belly would allow.

"But enough about me." He gave her a smile. In truth, the smile itself hadn't changed in the past eleven years. It was beautiful and charming and false. She'd almost fallen for that smile and a few sweet words once, and she was too savvy to fall for it now, no matter what the man behind the smile looked like. "How have you been?"

"Great," she said.

He reached across the table and laid his hand over hers. It was all she could do not to jerk that hand away and slap his face. "And is there…anyone special in your life?"

Sadie slowly drew her hand from Jason's, as the answer to that question popped into her mind. Damn. Double damn! The last thing she wanted was to get involved in even the smallest way with Truman McCain. But the answer was unmistakable.

"Yeah," she said honestly. "There is."

Jason drew away a little and his smile dimmed. He was obviously disappointed. "Oh." The smile flashed back quickly. "Of course, he's not here, and a woman gets lonely just like a man does. You look so hot tonight. For old times' sake…"

"If you finish that sentence I might have to hurt you," Sadie interrupted in her sternest voice.

Now Jason's smile was gone for good. His eyes, which had been friendly—and often more than friendly—flashed in a dark and almost threatening way. "If you're not interested, then why did you agree to have dinner with me?"

Again the truth. "Because I'm a complete idiot, that's why."

Jason leaned back in his chair. His eyes narrowed. "I get it. This is payback because I dumped you after the prom. You lead me on, tease me all night, then turn up your nose when I make a perfectly reasonable sugges- tion. There are lots of girls who'd like to be in your shoes tonight. It's really not fair of you to waste my time."

What an ego! "If I wanted payback for my old mis- takes, I could find a better way than enduring an end- less tirade about flea markets and fluorescent paint." She could actually think of several, at the moment. None of them legal. "And I never teased you, Davenport."

He scoffed at that one, and the look he gave her made her think the fight she'd wished for would take place at this very table. "You always were a cold bi…"

"Is something wrong?"

Sadie looked up, and there stood Truman. Tall and solid and unsmiling and absolutely beautiful. Heaven help her, the last thing she wanted or needed was a knight in shining armor, but oh…she had never been so happy to see anyone.

"Nothing's wrong," Jason said, his voice testy and biting.

Sadie stood and grabbed her purse off the back of the chair. "I could use a ride." She opened her purse and took out a ten-dollar bill, which was more than enough for her share of what Jason considered dinner. She dropped the bill on the table.

"Your piece is in the car," Jason said, not protesting in even the smallest way that she was paying for her own food and drink.

For a moment Sadie didn't know what he was talking about. Her gun was still snugly seated in her right boot.

"Of course, you haven't paid for it. I really should charge you full price, but since I already promised..."

"The fish!" Sadie said brightly.

"Yeah," Jason mumbled.

"Keep it, really. I'm such a cretin where the finer things are concerned. I have no appreciation for art."

His expression accused her of having no appreciation for other things. Like him.

"Good night." She walked to the door and Truman stayed directly behind her. When the crowd got thick he placed one steadying hand on the small of her back. She'd spent a long time getting strong enough to be confident without any guidance or steadying hands, but oh...it felt good.

The night was cool, and she stepped into the darkness with a real sense of relief. She saw Truman's pickup truck parked among the other trucks and cars in the gravel lot, and headed slowly in that direction. Truman didn't move his hand, and she didn't shake him off.

It was a real kick in the gut to realize that she still had feelings for Truman McCain. Was it love? Maybe, but probably not. Maybe it was just need wrapped up in fond memories or simple lust, or those hormones she had considered earlier this evening.

If she asked him…one more time…to make love to her, would he laugh at her again? She didn't think so. Would he refuse her? Unlikely. Just a couple of days ago she had felt the evidence that he wanted her pressing against her hip. Still, she was afraid to make the first move. She was scared of so little in this life. But being rejected by Truman…that fear was at the top of her list.

Sadie reached for the handle on the passenger door, but Truman's hand quickly covered hers. It was hard yet tender, the hand of a gentle man. She hadn't known many truly gentle men; she had even decided they didn't really exist, except in novels and movies and fairy tales.

And Garth, maybe.

Truman moved in close so his body was lightly touching her, his chest to her back, his cheek against her hair. With his free hand he moved her hair away and kissed her neck.

Sadie closed her eyes and felt as though she was drowning. That kiss danced through her entire body, it ignited flames deep inside her, flames that she'd been so careful to keep doused. Her breath caught in her throat, her heart began to pound. A knot of desire clenched in her gut. All because Truman's lips touched her neck.

"Sleep with me," he whispered into her ear. "You don't have to love me, and I swear I won't expect anything from you tomorrow." He dropped his hand from hers and rested it at her waist, warm and heavy. "I'm tired of wondering. I don't want to rely on my imagination anymore, and I want it to be you. Sleep with me. Please."

She turned in his arms. Those were the exact words she'd spoken to him when she'd been a sixteen-year-old virgin who was crazy in love with her cousin's best friend. "You remember?"

"Word for word." He traced her cheek with one long finger. "A man never forgets being propositioned by a beautiful woman."

"I should laugh at you." Instead of laughing, she rested her head against his chest. "We can't go back."

"I don't want to go back, Sadie. I want now."

He tipped her head back and kissed her. Like his hands, the kiss was soft and hard, gentle and arousing. She wasn't a sixteen-year-old virgin anymore, and she wanted this. She wanted one night with Truman Mc-Cain. She hadn't been lying when she'd told Jason she was involved. To the pit of her soul, she was involved with this man.

Maybe one night would chase away old demons once and for all, as well as the new and preposterous ideas that had taken up residence in her head.

"Yes," she whispered when he took his mouth from hers.

Chapter 7

"Were you expecting to bring me home tonight or are you actually a decent housekeeper?" Sadie asked as Truman switched on the lights that illuminated the kitchen and the great room.

"Would you be annoyed if I said a little of both?"

Sadie smiled widely. Man, she really should do that more often. She was always pretty, but when she gave him a true smile she took his breath away. Wouldn't do to let her know that much, he supposed.

"I guess not," she said as she casually scanned the room, the stairs that led to the open loft, the short hallway that led to his bedroom and the master bath. Silent approval softened her eyes. She liked it here, and for a reason Truman didn't care to explore he was glad.

"I didn't really expect to bring you home," he said as he linked his arm through hers and gently turned her to face him. He pushed aside an unruly curl that had fallen across her cheek. "But I did hope."

"You knew the date with Davenport would be a disaster."

"We are not going to stand here and talk about Jason Davenport."

She reached up and threaded her fingers through his hair, very lightly, very sexily. "Okay."

The kiss was like all the others: heat and desperation and promise. It had been a long time since he'd felt this way about a woman. Physical need was one thing, breathless craving was another altogether.

In a very basic way, he wanted to strip Sadie naked and take her here and now. But a part of him knew this wouldn't last, and he wanted everything to be perfect. Tomorrow morning she'd likely look at him and curse them both for a moment of weakness, and he'd never get another chance. The ABI would eventually catch whoever had killed Hearn, Sadie would be off the hook, and then she'd be gone. Maybe in another eleven years or so he'd run into her again. Maybe.

So he kissed her. He kissed her until she melted in his arms and her knees wobbled. He kissed her until she made those little noises low in her throat; little noises that told him she was losing control. He kissed her until he couldn't think of anything else, and neither could she.

They edged toward the hallway that led to the bedroom, still kissing, buttons here and there coming blindly undone as they took one step and then another. Sadie unfastened his shirt, one button at a time. He flicked open the button at her waist, and the zipper fell a little. Not a lot; not yet. And all the time, they kissed.

He didn't bother to turn on the overhead fixture as they stepped into the bedroom. There was enough light drifting from the main room to illuminate their path.

Sadie took her mouth from his to ask, "Do you have a…"

"Yeah." He slipped his hands beneath her sweater and pulled it over her head. The move ruffled the strands of hair that refused to be tamed, and he thrust his fingers into the dark curls and pulled her back in for another kiss, before sending the zipper on her trousers all the way down.

He'd laughed at her, surprised and bewildered, when she'd been sixteen and had offered herself to him.

He wasn't laughing now.

She had forgotten. Heaven help her, she had forgotten how good it felt to be touched by a man. Warmth and softness, sweat and hardness, trembling and anticipation and primal need. It was all right here, in the way their bodies came together.

Sadie pushed Truman's shirt off his shoulders. Nice shoulders, she noted before kissing them. Nice chest, too, with just enough muscle to be sexy and just enough hair to let her know he wasn't a kid anymore. He had a man's body, an athlete's body, hard and sculpted and a little bit worn around the edges.

He jerked down the quilt that covered his bed, revealing crisp white sheets beneath, and she sat on the side of the mattress, bouncing lightly as she landed. This was Truman's bed, where he slept every night. And tonight, he was going to sleep with her.

Her trousers couldn't come off until she removed

her boots and the pistol. Before she could get started, Truman grabbed one leg and tugged on a boot. Sadie laughed as she fell backward. The laughter bubbled up in her, uncontrolled and joyful. Anticipation rippled through her body. He removed her boot and the sock beneath before lifting the other leg.

"Careful," she said softly, her laughter fading.

With his hands on the boot, Truman lifted his eyebrows slightly.

"Gun," she explained.

He very gently removed the boot and the holster. "This is new," he said. "I've never had to disarm a woman in my bedroom before."

"Good." The word slipped out of her mouth before she had time to consider her response. This wasn't romance, it was sex. What she and Truman had was casual, not commitment. She shouldn't—*couldn't*—care if he'd ever disarmed a woman in his bedroom before tonight.

But she did.

Truman joined her on the bed and they undressed one another, slowly but with fingers that occasionally trembled. She hadn't trembled for any reason other than coming off an adrenaline rush in so long that she'd forgotten how it felt to spin out of control, to dance on the edge, hungry and heated and wanting. She was in danger of coming the moment he thrust inside her, at this rate.

Rolling away from her, Truman opened a bedside drawer. He had to reach into the back for a condom. She would never tell him, but she was glad those condoms weren't conveniently stashed at the front, as if he brought women into his bedroom every night.

The thought was foolish, but she didn't want to be just another woman. Not tonight.

It was reckless for her to be here, to offer herself not only physically but emotionally. Truman lowered himself to lie atop her, naked and hard, and she quit questioning herself. For once, she quit questioning herself.

Mouth to mouth was so fine it was almost enough. No man had ever kissed her quite this thoroughly. But Truman's hands on her skin felt so good, and the insistent thrum of her body told her the kiss wouldn't be enough for much longer. He touched her at the heart of that thrum, and she arched up into him as if she were still sixteen and madly in love and couldn't wait for him to be inside her.

No, when she'd been sixteen she'd had no idea what she'd been asking for when she asked Truman to make love to her. Now she knew exactly what she wanted….

She touched him, wrapped her legs around his hips and guided him to her. Into her. Holding on with her arms and her legs and pulling him into her body. She quivered, she clenched and unclenched and arched into him to draw him closer and deeper.

Truman made love to her as if he already knew her body intimately, and she responded. Each stroke took her closer to completion, but not too quickly. Each push took him a little bit deeper, until she was gasping every time he reached a new and untouched place.

She touched him with her trembling hands, and with a series of gentle swells she reached up to meet the sway of his hips. They fell into a rhythm without ever finding themselves in an awkward place. Their coming together was perfect, in a world that was flawed. How many perfect moments had she experienced in her life? Not many. None like this.

Eyes closed, heart pounding, she quit thinking and instead listened to the demands of her body. And what her body demanded was Truman.

He lifted her hips and pushed deep and she shattered, clenching around him and crying out softly. Her entire body was affected by the orgasm, and it came on waves that made her arch against him. Waves of pure joy washed through her, one and then another, until she could not breathe or speak or even move. He came with her; she felt it.

And then they melted down together, easing into the softness of the mattress.

Sadie didn't want to let Truman go just yet, so she didn't. She held on to him, with her thighs and her fingers. Her breath still wouldn't come right, and she quivered from head to toe.

In the back of her mind, she reminded herself that just because this was a stunningly beautiful moment, that didn't mean she could love him. It was just sex, and when she left Garth she wouldn't look back. Much.

She threaded her fingers in his hair. "Truman Mc-Cain, that was definitely worth waiting thirteen and a half years for."

He raised up and looked down at her. A small half-smile tilted the corners of his very fine mouth. "And the night isn't anywhere near over."

Truman wasn't done with her yet, and she certainly wasn't finished with him. This was the time for her to say something sweet, but not too sweet. Fond, but not clingy. Something that would tell him she cared—but not too much.

At a loss for the proper words, she finally settled for, "I'm starving. What have you got in the kitchen?"

Sadie wearing one of his plaid shirts and nothing else, standing at his kitchen counter making sandwiches, was enough to make Truman think odd and very bad thoughts. Things like: Why didn't she stay? Why did a woman who looked like Sadie Harlow want to be a private investigator, anyway? She could be anything she wanted to be. She could live anywhere, have any man...

Damned if she didn't have him by the nuts already.

He opened a bottle of wine, and Sadie carried the plate of sandwiches to the couch in the great room. They sat there—Sadie in the shirt that was halfway unbuttoned, he in a pair of boxers—and they sipped wine and ate the sandwiches. At first it was almost as if Sadie attempted to keep a distance, as if she didn't want to touch anymore now that the sex was over. And then she brushed against him once, and that distance disappeared.

She laid her hand on his arm when she asked about his brother, Kennedy. She leaned her head on his shoulder when she had finally had enough to eat and had placed the empty plate on the coffee table. For a little while they talked about unimportant things, like where he'd found the coffee table and Sadie's sudden craving for brownies and last week's college football games.

And then she reached down and laid her hand over his scarred knee and let it rest there.

"It really sucks, doesn't it," she said as she caressed the scars from the three old surgeries he'd had on that knee.

There had been a time when any mention of the injury had made him sad or angry, depending on the day and his mood. Tonight he could actually laugh. "Thank you. Most people either treat me like I have a handicap or else ignore the limp altogether. And you're exactly right. It sucks."

"But you're doing okay, right? Nice cabin, good job…"

"Respectable job," he corrected. "Maybe one day if I run for sheriff and win, then I'll have a *good* job."

Her body shifted against his, and damned if he wasn't ready to carry her back to the bedroom. Or take her here and now, on the couch, in the heat of passion that surged through him.

"There's something to be said for respectable," she said, settling against him and staring toward the window that looked out over the lake. There wasn't much to see at night, but the moon did sparkle on the water, and there was some beauty in that.

He slipped one hand into the mostly open shirt she wore and cupped one breast, brushing his thumb across the nipple that hardened at his touch. He had never been this comfortable with a woman. The touch was almost casual. Right and easy, as if his hands were simply drawn to her body because it was—in a way he had never experienced—his as well as hers.

"Since we're talking about jobs, can you tell me why on earth you do what you do?"

She didn't answer for a moment. "I'm good at it," she answered softly. "Isn't that enough?"

He should let it go right there. Push her back, open the rest of the buttons of his shirt, kiss her again.

But he didn't. "No, that's not enough. I did a little

checking around this week, while you were doing your best to ignore me. For God's sake, Sadie, The Benning Agency takes on some very dangerous jobs."

She didn't try to deny it or downplay the danger. "Yeah."

"You're right in the middle of it."

She hummed an affirmative answer.

"And you like it."

Sadie lifted her head and looked him in the eye. Her face was flushed, her lips full, her hair wild. "I do like it. Very much." She licked her lips, more nervous than seductive. "It's who I am now."

"I don't get it." A woman like this…she should have a man to hold her every night, a safe and warm place to call home, maybe a few kids. Truman knew his father's old-fashioned teachings were clouding his views on the matter. Not every woman wanted a man, a home and kids.

"I never had any control over my life," Sadie said softly. "Never. My father died, my mother died, I came here to Garth as a kid and was a fish out of water. After I left, things didn't get much better. I fell in love with the wrong man, he broke my heart, and once again I lost control of my life. I got so tired of letting other people tell me what to do and how to be, so I…I found myself taking another road."

"Having a gun doesn't put you in control."

Sadie almost smiled. "When you know how to use it…" She let the sentence hang there, unfinished.

She was so soft in his hands, even though she was taut with firm muscle and anything but weak. "I just want you to be careful, that's all."

She closed her eyes and leaned her head back. "Why?"

He didn't want to see her hurt. He didn't want to get the news through the grapevine, one day down the road, that Sadie Harlow had gotten her head blown off saving someone she'd never met. For the rush, for the paycheck, for her damned control.

But telling her that would probably send her running. He knew that much already. He grabbed her wrist in his hands and forced her gently back on the couch. "I have a feeling we could have this conversation all night and never agree."

She hummed again, affirmatively this time.

"I have better things to do with you tonight."

He got a full-blown, heart-stopping smile. "I'm glad to hear it."

He unbuttoned her shirt, and her body was laid out before him, toned and bare and gorgeous. He lowered his head and took one nipple into his mouth, drawing it deep and savoring, while Sadie threaded her fingers through his hair and held him there. She sighed. She bucked a little, her body waving up into his.

She wasn't in control now.

His mouth moved down slowly, tasting as he went. He spent a little time there at her belly button, and she laughed when he traced his tongue around it.

Sadie didn't laugh when he spread her thighs and placed his mouth against her, tasting her, teasing the nub at her entrance with his tongue. She came, quick and hard, bucking beneath him and crying out loud, shaking in his hands as the orgasm faded and she was left breathless. Again.

She sat up and pulled him close, reaching down to lay her hands on his erection and stroke. "Take me back to bed," she said, her voice husky. She pressed her shaking body to his. "I can't believe it, Truman, but I want you again."

And at least for tonight, he was going to give her everything she wanted.

Sadie made coffee, poured herself a cup, and stepped outside. Wearing Truman's shirt and a pair of worn drawstring pants she'd found in his chest of drawers, she carried her coffee down to the dock and sat, her bare feet dangling over the edge.

It was a morning fit for a postcard, with the trees around the lake red and gold and the rising sun glittering on the water. A cool wind chilled her bare feet, but Truman's clothes and the coffee cut the chill.

After the night they'd shared, her body ached. But oh, it was a good ache. A bone-deep, warm, loving ache. A night like last night could last a girl a long time in the memory department.

The memories would have to last. She did care for Truman. Too much. Much more than she wanted to care. But that caring couldn't stop her from living her life as she'd planned.

As she sat there, drinking in the quiet and the peace, she wished he lived in a forgettable place, or else that it was winter instead of autumn so the trees would be bare and ugly, and instead of a chill she'd have to suffer an icy blast to sit by the water.

Instead she was engulfed by a sense of belonging. That same sense Truman had talked about.

She adored her job and her friends and the life she'd made for herself. But this was home.

She'd fought it for so long, afraid to tie herself to any one place. When she wasn't tied down she didn't have anything to lose. No one could take away something that she didn't have.

Home. Family. Love. Truman.

She felt more than heard him behind her, and when he lowered himself carefully to sit beside her she scooted over to give him plenty of room. His arm around her shoulder felt so right, she was tempted to bolt.

"Good coffee," he said, sipping at the cup he'd poured himself.

She just hummed an answer, resting her head against his arm and staring at the lake. Like her, he'd pulled on a warm shirt and a pair of those drawstring pants. Sitting here, silent and just barely touching, was as intimate as making love in his bed, but in a different way. A scarier way.

"Are you okay?" he asked softly, after a few quiet moments had passed.

"Yeah. What's not to be okay about?"

"I woke up and you were gone, and I just wondered…"

"You thought I'd left," she finished for him.

"It crossed my mind."

She turned her face to him, and at her silent command—at her wish—he leaned down and kissed her.

"I'm too old to run away," she said, when he took his mouth from hers.

"Good." He kissed her again, deeper this time. It was a kiss that could very easily lead to more. Truman's mouth on hers was stirring and exciting, and it made her forget almost everything but the physical. She had butterflies in her stomach, and just a kiss made her tremble in all the wrong places. No, all the *right* places.

If she were younger, more reckless, just a little bit less in control, she'd make love to Truman here and now, with the autumn wind on their skin and the lake lapping just a few feet away.

But unless he had a condom in his pocket, that couldn't happen. The Benning Agency didn't exactly have a maternity plan.

Still, things quickly spun out of control. The kiss deepened, Truman's hands cradled her instead of a coffee cup, and she set aside her own empty cup to touch this man who made her question everything she wanted.

"I think I'm supposed to work today," she said between kisses.

"Didn't you hire someone to help?"

"I did." Kathy could handle it. Kathy and Jennifer, Mary Beth and Bowie and Aunt Lillian. Just for today, they could get along without her.

Truman grabbed her and hauled her onto his lap, and she laughed and squealed at the same time.

"Don't you dare let me fall into the water!"

"Afraid of the cold?"

"No."

He touched his nose to hers. "Afraid of the ghosts of Miranda and Sam?" he teased.

She held on tight. "No, I'm not afraid of the cold or of ghosts. I just…don't know how to swim." It was an embarrassing admission, but he really did need to know about her failing before he decided it would be cute to toss her in.

"You can't swim?" He backed away slightly to look her in the eye, and she could see his surprise.

Holding on to Truman while he held her made her feel secure—even here so close to the edge, with the deep water waiting a few feet away. "My mother refused to let me learn. My father drowned. Did you know that? We were living in Florida at the time, and he swam out into the Gulf to save a kid who had swum out too far. I was very young, so I don't remember my father, but when I was older Mom told me what happened. He managed to get the kid to safety, and then he went under and didn't come up. He drowned, so she was afraid to let me near the water even to learn how to swim."

"It never occurred to her that you'd be less likely to drown if you knew how to swim?"

She had to smile. "Logic and my mother rarely crossed paths."

He tightened his hold on her. "I guess we'd better go inside, then, and get you away from this nasty water."

"Good idea." She didn't rush to get out of his lap. "I have plans for you today, Truman McCain."

"Plans," he repeated.

She nodded and laid her lips on his throat, tasting and teasing. If all she could take away from Garth were memories, she might as well make the best memories possible.

Truman was heat and vitality and pleasure. He was an anchor in a world where Sadie had been adrift for so long she didn't know any other way.

Already she didn't want to leave.

Truman helped her to her feet then rose smoothly, with just the smallest hint of favoring his right leg. They walked toward the cabin arm in arm, but Sadie soon realized that her plans for the morning would have to wait. Before they reached the end of the pier she heard the car. Truman heard it, too. His head turned in that direction. It was too late to reach the house before whoever was approaching on the long driveway arrived, and besides…they were both too old to run and hide. At this point, she might as well give the town something else to talk about.

She'd wasted a lot of energy lately wondering what people here might think about her. Right now…she didn't care. It was a nice feeling.

When the car finally came into view she recognized it almost immediately, and so did Truman. The ABI investigator drove a two-year-old dark-green Impala that had been sitting in the parking lot of the Yellow Rose Motel for much of the past four days. What on earth did he want at this time of the morning? Surely any other questions he'd thought of could wait for a decent hour.

So much for starting the day in Truman's bed and staying there.

Evans's gaze went immediately to Sadie. "I thought I might find you here."

"Brilliant detective work," she said dryly. "What do you want?"

He turned his attention to Truman. "Has she been here all night?"

"Yeah."

Evans leaned against the fender and nodded, tired and weary and a little angry. "Could she have left during the night without your knowledge?"

Truman didn't answer right away, and when he finally did speak he said, "Unlikely. What happened?"

Evans didn't beat around the bush, and he didn't play cat and mouse. Straight to the point, that was his way. His eyes shifted to Sadie again, and he looked her in the eye.

"Jason Davenport was murdered early this morning."

Chapter 8

After a moment of stunned silence, Sadie responded with a hot, "If this is your idea of a joke…"

"I assure you, Miss Harlow, I don't joke about murder."

She went pale, but in true Sadie fashion there was no other display of emotion. "I saw Jason just last night."

"That's what I hear." The way Evans was looking at Sadie…even if he didn't think she murdered Davenport, he was definitely considering the possibility.

Truman took Sadie's arm. "Let's go inside and have some coffee. I'm sure you want to know what was said last night. I was there myself."

"I heard that, too." Evans pushed away from the car. The promise of coffee spurred him onward.

Truman was torn. He liked Sadie. Last night had been great, but it hadn't been nearly enough. There were moments when he thought they'd *never* get enough of each other. He even, in his weaker moments, felt a glimmer of something more. A connection. A sense of belonging as strong as the one he'd felt when he'd found this place.

But Sadie had been in town less than a week, and two men had ended up murdered. How far did she take her need for control? Did he know her at all? The girl, yes. The lover? Absolutely. But the woman? No. She'd been back in his life for a few days, and like everyone else she had secrets.

"You're not under arrest," Evans said to Sadie as he took the cup of coffee Truman offered him. "But I would be grateful if you'd answer some questions for me. If you feel like you need an attorney…"

"I don't," she snapped. "Ask away."

Evans leaned against the kitchen counter much the same way he had leaned against his car. It was a deceptively lazy pose. "Why don't you tell me what you and Jason Davenport argued about last night?"

Sadie's pose was much like the investigator's. She leaned against the counter in a casual stance, looking very much as if she belonged in this kitchen, in Truman's clothes. It was hard for her to look tough wearing clothes that were several sizes too large, but she managed. She didn't quite pull off the cool, though. She was wound so tight she looked as though she was about to pop.

"Jason thought he was going to get lucky because he gave me a discount on a wooden fish and drove me to a ratty bar in his clown car, where we shared wings and beer. I didn't agree."

"I see." Evans nodded. "This was at the Shamrock?"

"Yes, as you obviously already know."

The investigator wasn't bothered by Sadie's open hostility. "And later?"

"Later?"

"When you called him early this morning."

Sadie pushed away from the counter, all pretense of serenity gone. "I did *not* call him."

"That's not what I hear."

Sadie stepped toward Evans, and for a moment Truman wondered if he was going to have to throw himself between them to keep her from going to jail for assault. She stopped well short of swinging out.

"I left the Shamrock with Truman and I've been here all night. I didn't call anyone."

Again Evans shifted his focus to Truman. "Did you sleep?"

"Yeah," he answered honestly.

"Were you sleeping between two-thirty and five?"

Sadie turned to him, and he wondered what she expected him to say. Did she want him to lie for her? "Yes," he finally answered. "I was."

He looked into Sadie's eyes, which had gone dark, deep, and angry. After no more than two seconds, she took a step back. "You really think I'm capable of slipping out of here in the middle of the night and murdering someone, and then sneaking back into bed and pretending nothing happened."

"I didn't say…"

"You didn't have to." She spun and stalked toward the bedroom. "The look on your face and your lack of outrage at the suggestion that I kill any man who crosses me is enough."

"Sadie…"

"Don't you dare follow me," she snapped. "Haven't you already decided that pissing me off is dangerous?"

"I never said…"

She spun at the entrance to the hallway and glared at him. "No, you never said anything, did you?"

Sadie disappeared into the hallway. After a few seconds Evans muttered, in a weary voice, "Women."

Truman returned to the kitchen and poured himself another cup of coffee, his gaze on the dark brew as his mind spun this way and that. He'd known this thing with Sadie wouldn't last, but he sure as hell hadn't expected it to end this way. Suddenly and with more than a small dose of anger on her part.

Damn it, he wasn't anywhere near finished with her. There were so many questions he hadn't asked; so many things they hadn't done. He found he wasn't thinking only of the sex…good as it had been…but of other things. What made her laugh; what made her cry. Were her feet ticklish? Was she really a good shot or was that pistol mostly for show?

Had last night been as momentous for her as it had been for him, or was it just another one-night stand?

"You do know she didn't kill anybody," he said, as he and Evans waited for Sadie to return.

"At this point, all I know is two men she had public disagreements with have ended up dead."

"Sadie's too smart for this."

"She can be a freakin' genius, for all I care," Evans snapped. "We've had two murders in a week, in a county where it's been six years since the last homicide. And that was a man who caught his wife cheating, shot her, and then turned himself in. Am I supposed to believe that it's coincidence the murders began on Sadie Harlow's first night in town?"

Everything Evans had was circumstantial, but from what Truman had read, murders were usually cut and dried. People weren't framed. Serial killers were rare. Victims knew their killers and there was always, *always* a reason, especially when the murder was unnecessarily violent, as Hearn's had been.

"How was Davenport killed?"

Evans snorted. "Beaten to death with a big stick."

"Ouch."

"The coroner's report will read blunt trauma, I imagine, but beaten to death with a big stick is more accurate."

"Where?"

Evans pointed toward Truman's front door. "Two miles or so thataway, in a parking lot by the lake."

Very close to where he and Sadie had spent Tuesday night, sleeping in his truck.

"Where did the call come from?"

"Don't know yet. People are on it. Davenport didn't have caller-ID, so we have to go through the phone company."

Sadie stormed out of the hallway, wearing her own rumpled clothes and a fiery expression. She didn't look at him, but kept her eyes on Evans.

"Am I under arrest?"

"No."

"Can I have a ride to town anyway?"

"Sadie, I'll…" Truman began.

She spun on him, and looked him square in the eye. "Don't think that I'll ever get in that truck with you again, McCain. Evans I understand. He's doing his job. If I was him I'd suspect me too, I guess. But you... Last night you slept with me, and this morning you can actually stand there and look at me as if you're seriously considering the possibility that I came home to Garth and killed two men in five days." She spun around and glared at Evans. "If I was going to kill anyone it would be Truman McCain, so if he doesn't turn up dead real soon you can take me off your list of suspects because it proves that I have an abundance of restraint."

"I'm afraid it doesn't work that way," the ABI investigator said.

Evans and Sadie headed for the doorway, Evans dragging, Sadie on fire. When Sadie opened the door Truman took a move in that direction. One step. She didn't look back, but somehow she knew he had made a move to follow and she spoke.

"Stay where you are, McCain. It's over."

Saturdays were always busy, and for once Sadie was happy to work at the café. She needed to stay busy, to get her mind off what had happened last night. And this morning. Of course, people had begun to talk, and she was the recipient of more than a few suspicious and curious stares. None of them bothered her the way Truman's questioning eyes had.

Kathy was a very good waitress, and had very quickly fallen into a routine with Bowie and Aunt Lillian and Mary Beth. Aunt Lillian had found her a uniform that actually fit, and her name was neatly embroidered over the right breast. The customers seemed to like her well enough. She was sweet. Sweet

and innocent and undeserving of whatever some worth-
less man had done to send her running. And even now,
when Sadie's mind was spinning, there was something
naggingly familiar about that pretty girl.

It was probably something simple. She was related
to someone Sadie had gone to school with, or she looked
like a regular café customer, or she just had one of those
familiar faces.

It was fifteen minutes to closing time, and there were
just a few customers left in the café. Two fishermen in
a booth by the window, and a single older woman at a
table in the center of the room. Mary Beth and Aunt Lillian were long gone, and Bowie was cleaning the
kitchen.

Kathy and Sadie cleaned the booths and the counter,
and Kathy had already started refilling the sugar canis-
ters to prepare for Monday morning.

"Are you all right?" the girl asked as Sadie moved
near, her voice low so that none of the remaining customers would hear.

"Fine and dandy," Sadie said in a voice that made it
clear nothing was fine *or* dandy.

Kathy cast her eyes down. "I didn't mean to pry. I just
thought if you wanted to talk…I'm not going anywhere."

Sadie Harlow didn't cry on anyone's shoulder. Not
ever. It was pathetically girlie and needy, and that's not
who she was. Not any more. But oh—if she didn't get
some of this out of her system she was going to lose it,
and given that she was suspected of two violent killings
that probably wouldn't be wise.

"You've heard the rumors, I suppose," she said
reluctantly.

"About that guy who was murdered in 119? Please. I'm sure everyone knows that you didn't kill anyone. How ridiculous."

Sadie turned away as hot tears sprung to her eyes. *How ridiculous.* That's all she'd wanted from Truman, this morning when Evans had shown up and spouted his accusations. Instead he'd told the investigator that he'd been asleep during the time in question, and then he'd looked at her as if he were actually considering the possibility that he'd made love to a murderer last night.

She was as angry at herself for expecting more as she was at Truman for not defending her like the knight in shining armor that she did *not* want.

"Have you ever *not* been disappointed by a man?" Sadie asked softly. "Have you ever gotten involved with a man who didn't eventually make you regret the day you met him?"

Kathy sighed. "No. Not really. Bowie is very nice," she added brightly.

"Yeah, well, talk to his ex-girlfriends and see how nice they think he is." Sadie wiped down her booth with extra energy. "I know there are people out there who meet and fall head over heels and get married and everything is just hunky dory all the time. I know it happens. Maybe some of us are just not supposed to…to…"

"Fall in love?" Kathy supplied when Sadie faltered.

Sadie almost swallowed her tongue trying to answer. "No! Not love. Not…that." She couldn't possibly love Truman McCain. "It just seems like men are always overly eager to disappoint, know what I mean?"

"Yeah," Kathy said softly.

The two fishermen sitting by the window finally left.

Bowie had just finished in the kitchen, and he took their money at the cash register and made change. The men left and Bowie, with a quick wave and a "See you Monday," was right behind them. That left just the two pink-clad waitresses and one old woman who continued to sip at her coffee.

"Some man disappointed you, right?" Sadie kept her voice low, and for a moment she wondered if Kathy even heard her. The girl kept cleaning, and she didn't look up. "You can talk to me, if you'd like. Maybe I can help."

Kathy headed toward the cash register when she spotted the last customer rise with check and cash in hand. She intercepted the older lady, smilingly gave change, and then locked the door behind her. When she returned to cleaning the table with a vengeance, Sadie decided Kathy just wanted to drop the subject. Not that she could blame her.

Sadie mumbled to herself as she cleaned. Did she really look like a killer? Not just someone who might dispose of a bad man who had a gun trained on her or one of the guys, but a cold-blooded killer. Truman apparently thought so, and so did Evans. Again, Evans's suspicions didn't bother her nearly as much as Truman's did.

Why had she been so foolish as to expect better of him? Expecting better always led to disappointment.

After a few minutes, Kathy sat down at a booth near Sadie. She played with her fingernails, stared at the tabletop, and finally lifted her head to look at Sadie. Realizing that Kathy was waiting for her, Sadie took a seat on the other side of the booth. For a long while Kathy remained silent, but something in the air, and in the pretty girl's eyes, kept Sadie riveted to her seat.

"There is no abusive husband or boyfriend looking for me," Kathy said quickly.

"Then why are you here? I know you're running from something."

Kathy stared at the tabletop again and placed her hands in her lap. "I'm in trouble," she said, her voice so low Sadie could barely hear her. "Real bad trouble."

Her face was so pale, Sadie didn't doubt that she was telling the truth. "I'll help, if I can."

Kathy shook her head. "Thanks, really, but... No one can help. It's too late. I messed up everything..."

"Tell me," Sadie said, gently commanding. Nothing was so bad that it couldn't be fixed.

Kathy placed her hands on the tabletop and threaded her fingers together, gripping them tightly. She did not look Sadie in the eye. "When I was seventeen, my stepfather decided that beating me wasn't enough to satisfy him anymore. He didn't touch me at all while Mom was alive, but once she was gone..." She took a deep breath and exhaled slowly. "Everything that went wrong, every disappointment, he took it out on me. I learned how to duck, and how to hide when he was in a mood, but I didn't have any place to go so I stayed. One night he came home mad about something that had happened at work, and I didn't get out of his way fast enough. He... he raped me."

Outrage flew up in Sadie, as if the blood boiled inside her veins.

"I didn't have anywhere to go," Kathy continued. "My brother, the only other family I had, I'd just found out that he was dead, too. We got a...a letter. I didn't know what to do, so I've been running ever since." Her voice was small, as if she couldn't bear to hear the words she spoke.

Sadie reached across the table and placed her hands over Kathy's. The poor girl trembled. A few sentences, and Sadie's own troubles seemed not so bad. "Oh, honey. If you want to go back home and face him, I'll be with you every step of the way. I'll protect you from your stepfather and I will make sure he goes to jail for the rest of his…"

"He's dead," Kathy said softly. She slowly lifted her head. "I killed him."

Evans had set up an office of sorts at the Sheriff's headquarters in Garth, claiming a corner and a small desk and a phone. Sheriff Wilks wasn't territorial. He was a political animal, and all he cared about was that the murders in his county were solved. He didn't care who solved them. His own investigators were unaccustomed to such violent cases, so they all made the ABI investigator welcome and gave him whatever he asked for.

Apparently they had all heard about where Sadie Harlow had been located this morning. When Truman walked into the office, all eyes turned in his direction. Instead of the usual round of friendly greetings, he was met with silence.

He headed straight for Evans, who sat at the desk he'd claimed as his own. Without looking up, Evans said, "Your coffee is better." A cup of unnaturally dark brew in a foam cup sat near his elbow.

"Yeah, I know. Did you trace the phone call?"

Evans glanced up. "I really shouldn't be telling you any of this, you know. I shouldn't be talking to you at all."

"Maybe I can eliminate Sadie as a suspect altogether. Tell me when and from where that call was made, and maybe I can clear a few things up." He could account for her at two, and not long after five he'd come awake for a few minutes and she'd been lying beside him.

"Why should I believe you? You're obviously thinking with your..."

"I won't lie to you, not even to cover for Sadie."

Evans nodded slightly and considered Truman closely—as if he were a suspect himself. "The call was made from a phone booth at the gas station near the park where the body was found. Elmo's or..."

"Elton's," Truman said crisply.

"That's it. The call was made at two-fifty-four. Davenport was at home drinking with a buddy, still moaning about the outcome of his date with Miss Harlow and the state of women in general, when he got the call."

"How does that point to Sadie, exactly?"

"His buddy could tell that it was a woman's voice on the other end of the line, and a very surprised and happy Davenport called the woman Sadie. He ended the phone call quickly and then told his friend that he had to leave. The body was found at six, in that park on the opposite side of the lake from your place. I don't have the coroner's report just yet, but even I could tell that he'd been dead a few hours."

Logistically, she could've done it. Sadie could've left him sleeping, taken his truck, made the call, killed Jason Davenport and been back in bed by five.

But he couldn't believe it. She was tough, she was angrier than she'd let anyone know. But she wasn't a psychopath.

"She didn't do it."

"You already said you were asleep between two-thirty and five."

"I was, but…"

"That's more than enough time for her to sneak out, take your truck, make the call and kill Davenport, then slip back into bed."

"She didn't."

Evans was not convinced. "I'm going to want to have a look at your truck."

A flash of anger rose up in Truman. "Go ahead. You're not going to find anything."

Wilks sauntered out of the office, his chin lifted high as he took on that pose he always adopted when he wanted to look important. He knew Truman had aspirations to take his job one day, thanks to Abby McCain's glowing words about her son and his future, and he didn't like it. Not at all. "McCain," he said, hooking his thumbs in his belt and joining the conversation uninvited.

"Sheriff," Truman said softly.

"I hear you've gotten yourself knee-deep in the wrong side of a murder investigation."

"Is that what you hear?"

"Yep."

Evans remained silent. He decided to leaf through some papers on his desk and ignore the exchange taking place above his seated position.

"Sadie didn't do anything…"

"Regardless of your obviously biased opinion, you are knee-deep in a mess of horse hockey, deputy." Wilks offered his hand. "I'm going to have to ask for your badge and gun, at least until this investigation is done."

Truman took the gun from his holster and handed it over, then reached for his badge and did the same.

"If it turns out your lady friend is innocent, then we'll talk about you getting these back. Until then…"

"Keep 'em," Truman said as he walked away from the sheriff and the ABI investigator. "I'm done."

Before he reached his truck, Evans was right beside him. Apparently the investigator was capable of moving much more quickly than he usually did.

"I think I'll have a look at that truck of yours now."

"Have at it," Truman snapped.

Evans slipped on a pair of cotton gloves and opened the driver's side door. He very cautiously looked around, searching the seats and the floorboard and behind the seat for anything that might be called incriminating. Truman stood back and let him look to his heart's content.

He didn't need the money from his job as deputy. For a few years he'd made big bucks playing football, and he'd been smart enough to invest it well instead of spending it all, even though Diana had very much wanted to spend every dime he made. She'd gotten more than she deserved when she'd left him, settlement-wise, but still, he had a nice little bit tucked away.

No, he didn't need the money, but he did need the purpose the job gave him. The feeling of being a part of something larger than his own ego. After losing his career and his trophy wife, he'd felt at loose ends for a long time. The job as deputy and the occasional aspirations to sheriff had given him a sense of purpose again.

And now that was gone. Until Evans turned his attentions to a suspect besides Sadie, he was stuck in the middle of this mess. Knee-deep, Wilks had said more than once.

He should've approached Sadie with the same detachment he'd called upon when dealing with women since the divorce. Detached sex was easy, but when a man started wondering what would make a woman laugh and cry he was in too damned deep.

Finding nothing in the cab of the truck, Evans turned to the bed. He lowered the gate and stepped up and inside…no small feat, since he was not a small or an athletic man. He studied every speck of dirt as he made his way forward, and sidestepped a few large pieces of mud along the way.

When Evans reached the small lockbox, he looked to Truman. "Key?"

Truman was shuffling through the keys on his keychain, looking for the right one, when Evans whistled low and reached into the small space between the lock box and the side of the truck bed. He came up with a single gardening glove, which was muddy and stained with something in addition to mud.

Blood.

Chapter 9

At first she thought the black pickup truck that pulled into the parking lot was a new customer for the motel, or someone who'd forgotten that the café closed at two. It was almost upon her before she saw the driver's face.

A very angry Truman McCain stared at her through the windshield, as he parked the truck not three feet from Sadie. She turned and walked into the room she'd been about to clean, ignoring him completely.

She heard the truck door slam. Hard. Next thing she knew Truman was in the room with her. At least he had the good sense to keep his distance.

She stripped the sheets off the unmade bed with a vengeance. "New truck?" she asked, after a few moments of uncomfortable silence.

"A loaner. Mine's been impounded."

She snapped her head around to look at him. No, he

wasn't kidding. He had never looked less like he was kidding. "Why?"

"Take a wild guess." He didn't lean against the doorjamb, he didn't smile, his blue eyes didn't twinkle.

"I'm sure they won't keep it long. There's nothing to find."

"Nothing except a bloody glove in the truck bed," he snapped.

Sadie dropped the sheets. "That's not possible."

Truman walked toward her, and the small room suddenly felt smaller. Closer. Warmer. "My truck has been impounded, my cabin is off limits until the ABI has finished searching for more blood, and the sheriff asked for my gun and badge this afternoon."

"I'm so sorry," she said softly. "I never intended…" She'd been so angry with him, but looking at him now she could only feel regret that she hadn't just mucked up her own life; she'd mucked up Truman's as well. "I didn't do it."

"I know that," he snapped. "Don't you think I know that?"

She shook her head.

"Someone is setting you up, Sadie, and things don't look good. Evans isn't even looking at anyone else for the murders."

"But I didn't…"

"You have motive, you have opportunity, and damned if you don't have the attitude."

"Wait just a minute," she said, stepping toward him. Attitude? She'd show him attitude. "I don't appreciate you coming in here tossing out all the reasons why I make such a great murder suspect. I'm not an idiot and I'm not blind."

Truman didn't back down or away as she advanced, but grabbed her wrist and held on tight. "The way I see it we have two choices. We can sit back and wait for Evans to arrest you, or we can find the killer ourselves. The choice is yours, Sadie. After all, it's your head on the chopping block."

She could call Benning and have the entire team— well, whoever was available—here in a matter of hours. They took care of their own, and the Major had the resources. But Sadie didn't want to go that route, not immediately, anyway. If she and Truman could take care of this mess on their own, no one she worked with would ever have to know that she was foolish enough to come home and get herself embroiled in not one but *two* murders. She definitely didn't want them coming face-to-face with Truman.

They sat at the small table in Truman's motel room. Since his cabin was off limits, he'd taken up residence here for the time being.

"We need to find Conrad," she said. "He must've seen something Monday night that spooked him, and he ran. We need to know what he saw."

"What if he's dead, too?" Truman asked. "If the killer knows he was seen going into that room, it's definitely a possibility. Then there's always the possibility that Conrad killed Hearn, for some reason we haven't uncovered yet."

Sadie shot out of her chair and began to pace in the small space that allowed such movement. "Does anything tie Hearn and Davenport together?"

"You mean, anything beside you?"

She spun and stared down at Truman. "Yes. Anything besides me."

"I don't know. Hearn, the missing Conrad, Davenport. This is a small town, Sadie, but I swear, I don't think those three knew one another at all. They ran in three very different crowds."

"There has to be something!"

Truman remained calm. "We need to go back to Hearn. This started with him. And don't discount the possibility that there are two killers and two motives, and whoever killed Davenport just chose this opportunity because you're already under suspicion in Hearn's murder and they saw a way to muddy the trail. The bloody glove was obviously planted in my truck to make sure Evans doesn't look at anyone but you for this."

"Great. I'm a patsy."

"Sit," Truman ordered.

"I can't."

"Sit. You're making me nervous."

Instead of sitting again at the table between the wide window and the double bed, she perched on the end of the bed. The mattress dipped. She tapped her toes nervously on the carpet. From this vantage point, she didn't have to look at Truman.

Like it or not, it still stung that he had been slow to come to her defense. He had, eventually, but the look in his eyes this morning…it stayed with her. That look had been a reminder that she couldn't rely on anyone else. Professionally, yes. She trusted the other Benning agents with her life, and even now, working with Truman, she trusted him to do his best. But personally? Never.

"It's going to be all right," he said, his voice oddly

and unexpectedly soothing. He hadn't been this even-tempered since some point last night, when they'd both been sated and unnaturally happy and drugged with afterglow. He certainly hadn't been so calm when he'd stormed into a different motel room this afternoon.

"Is it?"

"Sure. Have faith, Sadie Mae."

She didn't scold him for calling her Sadie Mae, since there was teasing in his voice and he so obviously meant to distract her.

"I don't." She didn't have faith in anything, and hadn't had for a very long time.

"I know," he said softly.

She tried to explain, even though she didn't owe Truman any explanations. "If you expect the worst, you're never disappointed."

"That's a sad way to spend your life."

"Yeah. It is. But it works for me."

Truman crawled onto the bed. The mattress dipped, the bed creaked. And when he put his arms around her she didn't push him away. She placed her hands on his strong forearms and soaked up his body heat and the comfort he offered.

He lowered his head and kissed her shoulder. "It's going to be okay, Sadie."

She wanted to believe him. She wanted so very badly to believe… "Do you actually think that the two of us can find the real killer and then everything will magically go back to the way it was?"

"I don't want everything to go back to the way it was."

Her heart skipped a beat. "What about your job?"

"I'm running for sheriff in the next election. I had

planned to wait a few years, but Wilks needs to go sooner rather than later."

"You'll make a good sheriff." But he wouldn't get elected if she was charged with murder and his name was attached to hers.

She wanted to stay here, get lost in these warm, strong arms and let him tell her again and again that everything would be all right. She wanted to sleep with him again, here in this bed. Last night she'd slept so well with Truman beside her.

But she wasn't going to stay in Garth when this was all over and done. And the more involved she and Truman were, the more this catastrophe of a relationship would stain his reputation.

He moved his mouth to her neck, and a shudder whipped down her spine. She closed her eyes and savored it before whispering, "I can't do this."

"Of course you can. We can't start investigating until tomorrow morning. Tonight…"

She slipped out of his arms and stood, and he didn't try to stop her. "No. What happened with us last night, that's over. We're not…dating, McCain. We were both lonely so we got a little old business out of our systems."

"Old business?" he repeated in a dangerously low voice.

"Old business."

She backed toward the door. "You know, I really don't need you to investigate anything. I'll check around myself, and if I don't find what I'm looking for in a couple of days I'll call my boss and he'll put a couple of the guys on it. With the resources the Benning Agency has they'll get this cleared up in no time."

"Why not call them tonight?" Truman asked, his voice tight.

"I'd rather wait. Just a few days."

"Don't want them to know what you've stepped in here, do you?"

"Not really," she admitted as she backed to the door and laid her hand on the knob.

Truman didn't chase her, and he didn't try to change her mind. He reclined on the bed, but he didn't take his eyes off her. "One of these days you're going to have to trust somebody. It might as well be me."

Without responding, Sadie opened the door and stepped into the night, glad for the slap of fresh cool air on her hot face.

Old business. What a load of bull.

Truman called his mother and told her where he was. Good thing he called when he did. She'd heard the rumors and was in a state of panic. It took him a good fifteen minutes to convince her that he was not moving back in with her until his cabin was released.

When that was done he called Kennedy. He didn't want his brother getting the story from their mother. With the slant she was sure to put on it, Kennedy would feel like he had to show up to offer support. The last thing Truman wanted was an entourage.

What he wanted was Sadie Harlow in his bed, but she obviously had no desire to repeat what had happened last night.

Old business.

When he'd finished talking to family, Truman called a few deputies, friends who would stand by him if he asked them to. He thanked them for their offers of help but declined. He didn't want to drag any of them down with him.

He was on his own.

Kathy was gone. She'd obviously regretted her confession and decided to run before Sadie used what she knew as a bargaining tool with the ABI.

No jury in the world would convict Kathy, not if the story she'd told Sadie yesterday afternoon was true. Apparently the stepfather had assaulted her in a rage, that one time, and when he'd come back for more—on the kitchen table, no less—Kathy had picked up a cast-iron skillet and hit him over the head.

She'd run from the house, scared and in a panic, her mind on one thing only. Escape. But when she'd called a friend a couple of weeks later, she'd gotten the news of her stepfather's demise. She'd been running and hiding ever since.

After she'd heard the tale, Sadie had tried to convince Kathy to turn herself in. Running and constantly looking over her shoulder was a lousy way to live, and there would be no end to it until Kathy faced the past. Sadie had even offered to make the trip home with the girl, as soon as this ridiculous mess in Garth was cleared up and she was free to go.

And now, Kathy was gone. Her room was clean, and she'd left her uniform on the bed and a note on the front counter. The uniform was neatly folded. The note read simply, "Sorry. K.C."

Sorry. If Sadie didn't have more pressing matters on her mind she'd chase the girl down today and try to talk some sense into her! Kathy wouldn't have a normal life until she put the past behind her.

But she didn't have time to chase Kathy. And besides, what did Sadie Harlow know about a normal life?

Sitting in her room above the motel office, she looked down at Truman's room and the loaner truck parked by his door. Was what had happened truly old business, as she'd told him? Did she feel a fondness for him because they'd slept together and it was so good? Or was there more?

She'd never get the chance to find out. The further away from Truman she stayed, the better off he'd be. Hadn't she done enough to him already?

He'd be a good sheriff. He fit in here. Everybody loved him, and eventually they'd forget that he'd made the mistake of sleeping with Sadie Harlow.

One night was forgivable. A true involvement—a relationship, a commitment, love—that could ruin him.

Aunt Lillian returned from church, still pale thanks to all the excitement in her usually sedate life. Sadie had stirred up Lillian's life as well as Truman's. The woman would've been better off if she'd never agreed to take her sister's kid in. She would definitely have been better off if she'd called on someone else for help when she needed it. Anyone else.

Her footsteps on the stairs were unusually slow and heavy. Of course she had been subjected to gossip and curious stares at church. The gossip and the stares would've hurt, and considering what was going on, Lillian had surely expected to be the object of some curiosity. But she'd gone to church anyway, because she always attended and she took great comfort from it, and no one was going to take that comfort away from her.

There was a soft knock on Sadie's door. Before she had a chance to respond, the door opened and Lillian stepped inside. She closed the door behind her, softly but soundly.

"I'll leave," Sadie offered without turning to look at her aunt.

"You'll do no such thing," Lillian responded.

"But I know people are talking…"

"People are morons."

Sadie turned in her chair to look up at her aunt in her Sunday best, complete with a small navy blue hat that matched her dress and shoes. Lillian had taken special care with her appearance this morning, knowing that she'd face closer scrutiny than usual.

Lillian was strong in a way Sadie could never be.

"I'm going to find the killer, and then I'm going to get out of town," Sadie said. "I won't come back, this time. I promise."

"Don't you dare say such a thing," Lillian snapped. "This is your home…"

"I don't have a home," Sadie interrupted. "I never did."

Lillian lifted her chin and her face paled, and Sadie felt a rush of regret. Her aunt had tried to make this home; if it didn't work, it was Sadie's own fault. Not Lillian's.

"Maybe you don't consider this your home," Lillian said smartly, "but what about Truman? Are you just going to walk away from him?"

"Yes." A tickle of something unwanted traveled down her arms, down her spine.

"That's hardly fair."

Sadie didn't want to shock and dismay her aunt, but

she couldn't have the woman playing matchmaker and thinking that there was more to Sadie and Truman than met the eye.

With all the stories that were flying about, it would be impossible to deny what had happened. But she could put her own slant on things. "Truman was just for fun. That's all. Recreation. A convenient diversion."

"Bull hockey," Lillian cracked, her voice harsh.

Sadie actually smiled. "It is possible to have a completely casual relationship with a man in this day and age."

"Not for you," Lillian said. "You're too much like your mother, you know. She was so fragile when it came to her emotions."

"I am *not* fragile, not in any way," Sadie protested.

"I see the way you look at Truman," Lillian argued, "and I see the way he looks at you."

"That's just physical."

Lillian shook her head. "Tell me the truth, Sadie Mae. How many men have you slept with?"

"Aunt Lillian!"

"Woman to woman, and if you don't tell me the truth I'll know it."

For a moment Sadie sat there with her mouth tightly closed and her face expressionless. Lillian gave no sign of giving up.

"Three," Sadie finally said.

"Loved all three of them, didn't you?"

Sadie swallowed. "At the time…" Oh, God, she was about to admit that she was actually in love with Truman McCain. "Yes. But I always choose badly," she said. "I let my heart and my body tell me where to go, and they're always wrong."

"Not this time," Lillian said softly. "Don't let an old mistake rob you of a chance at real happiness."

Sadie looked out the window, unable to meet her aunt's telling stare. "My happiness doesn't matter. If I…I could ruin Truman's chance at having what he wants."

"How do you know what he wants?"

Because I know the man to the pit of his soul. "The sheriff's office, a home, babies named after presidents…"

"And how are you going to keep him from getting those things?"

"Just by being here," Sadie answered softly.

"Hogwash," Lillian said. "After his exciting life blew up in his face, Truman McCain came back to Garth and put on a happy grin for everyone. He said all the right things whenever anyone asked him about his knee or the divorce or what it was like not to be a star anymore. He got himself a job and made some new friends, and he even went out on a few dates."

"See? He's doing fine."

"He is not doing fine," Lillian cracked. "Until you came back home, there wasn't a speck of fire in the boy. I remember him as a teenager. He was full of fire, back in those days, and since he came back here I wondered if the fire still simmered inside him. It does, I know that now."

"But…"

"But nothing," Lillian interrupted. "You woke him up, Sadie. You lit that fire. And now you're just going to walk away? That's hardly fair."

"He'll be better off without me. Fire is…highly overrated."

"You really are just like your mother," Lillian said without heat. "She would never listen to me, either. You don't know how hard I tried to get her to move here after your father died."

How different would her life have been if she'd lived here all her life? She didn't even want to contemplate.

"She wouldn't have any of it. Stubborn woman, she was determined to make it on her own, and the costs be damned."

Sounded familiar. Horribly, deeply familiar.

"You don't talk about her much," Sadie said.

"Neither do you."

"It still hurts." That shouldn't be the case, not after all these years, but it was true.

"I know. It hurts me, too." Lillian pulled up a chair and sat beside Sadie. For a few moments they both stared out the window, and it was as oddly comfortable as lying in Truman's arms.

It was Lillian who spoke first. "You're going to investigate Aidan Hearn, aren't you?"

Sadie nodded, glad to turn her thoughts to something she could pretend to control. "Yeah. I'll start with him and see what I can find. I already suspect that he was coming here to meet a woman. I hear he had quite the reputation as a ladies' man."

"Yes, he did."

Sadie scoffed. "I never met Hearn face to face, not alive that is, but his picture didn't exactly show a good-lookin' man. And he was a big guy. Not a fifty-nine-year-old Adonis, if you know what I mean."

Lillian nodded gently. "Aidan wasn't the most handsome man in the world, that's true. And he had terrible eating habits, which had begun to show on him in the past few years."

Aidan?

"But he could make a woman feel like she was beautiful, even if her days of true beauty were long gone. He knew how to make a woman think, at least for a few hours, that nothing else in the world mattered. He was exciting and passionate and…yes, he had his flaws, and they were big ones. But I don't regret for a minute…"

Sadie no longer looked into the parking lot. Her eyes were riveted to Aunt Lillian's face. A few tears trickled down the woman's pale cheeks.

"You…" Sadie choked.

"Yes. Thirteen months after Jimmy passed, Aidan and I became intimately involved."

Sadie's stomach did a sick flip. "You're pulling my leg."

Lillian shook her head. "No, I'm very serious."

"But…he was married." That wasn't the only problem with the scenario, but it was the one that shocked her most. Aunt Lillian had always been so devoted to her husband, and she was such a fan of the institution of marriage.

Tears dribbled down Lillian's cheeks, ruining her carefully applied makeup. "I tried to rationalize. His marriage was not a good one, at least…that was what he led me to believe. Their children were grown and gone from home, and it's not like I expected Aidan to leave his wife for me. We just had really great…."

"Please don't say another word," Sadie said quickly.

Lillian looked at Sadie and smiled shakily. For an instant Sadie saw a woman who was more than a mother and an aunt. She saw an attractive woman who had been lonely and vulnerable after her husband's passing. A woman who had loved, just as Sadie had loved.

"Do you think a woman passes the age where she

longs to be touched?" Lillian asked, her voice soft but strong. "I knew the affair was wrong, but…Aidan swept me off my feet. He held me, and he loved me, and he made me feel like a beautiful woman. I was so lonely, Sadie. I missed Jimmy so much…" Her voice broke. "So many times I went to Aidan intending to end the relationship, but I couldn't do it."

"Were you with him the night he died?"

"No! We hadn't been seeing each other for months. It's been almost a year, in fact."

"Why did it end?" Sadie asked.

Lillian gathered her strength. "It ended because I fell in love with him, and I just couldn't bear to carry on in secret any more, knowing that all we'd ever have was an afternoon twice a week, and perhaps a night together when his wife went to visit her sister in Atlanta. After I fell in love with him, the relationship began to seem…untidy."

"Did he love you?"

Lillian shook her head. "No. But he was very possessive, and he was unhappy that I ended the affair. He let me know within a few days that he'd replaced me with a younger woman, one who was prettier and firmer and smarter…"

"That ass!" Sadie snapped.

"He was very insecure," Lillian said kindly. "For months he called and dropped by and tried to convince me to meet with him again. When he realized that I wasn't going to let him back into my life, he decided to punish me by calling in the loan. That's why I asked you to speak with him. I couldn't bear to sit down with him over money matters, and I knew he would have to behave reasonably with you where business is concerned.

So you see, I am entirely responsible for this mess you're in."

"No…" Sadie reached out and took Lillian's hand.

"Yes, this is all my fault." Her lower lip trembled. "And a man I once loved is dead, and I can't even mourn him because I don't want Jennifer to know that I betrayed her father with another man."

"She wouldn't think such a thing."

"Yes, she would. Jennifer adored her father. I don't think she'd accept his death as an excuse for me to replace him in my bed. Besides, letting the news of my affair with Aidan out now wouldn't serve any purpose. It would hurt his wife, who I discovered too late was not the monster Aidan painted her to be. Worse, it would hurt Jennifer." Her chin trembled. "This is so hard, Sadie. I can't even cry for him."

Sadie reached out and pulled her aunt's head into her shoulder. "Of course you can cry for him," she said softly. "Here and now. I promise not to tell."

As the older woman cried on Sadie's shoulder, Sadie whispered words of comfort and thought of how she'd mourn if anything happened to Truman. The very idea sent an unpleasant chill up her spine.

A part of her could well imagine staying here in Garth, living in that cabin and making love every night, having babies and naming them after presidents, being a proper sheriff's wife.

She did care about Truman. But she didn't know if she cared enough about him to give up her life for him. That would take love…and she didn't believe in love anymore. The best thing she could do for him was to stay far, far away.

Chapter 10

"What are you doing here?"

Truman turned his head toward the office doorway. Sadie was dressed conservatively today, in a pleated navy skirt and low heels and a red sweater. The pleats were convenient, when it came to concealing a thigh holster.

"I'm talking to Rhea," he answered. "What are *you* doing here?"

"I have an appointment," she said tersely.

"Oh," Rhea said, her voice whiny. "Mr. Elliot had to cancel that appointment. I can reschedule you for Wednesday."

For a moment, Sadie looked as though she wanted to argue. But the fight in her eyes died quickly. "Sure. Why not? It's not like I'm going anywhere before Wednesday rolls around."

Rhea penciled in a time for Sadie on Wednesday afternoon. Sadie turned to leave, in an oddly obedient way, and then she pivoted in a manner that made her skirt swish and tease. "McCain, may I speak with you? Outside?"

Truman smiled at Rhea, told her they'd finish their conversation later, and followed Sadie to the parking lot.

They had both left their vehicles in the back lot, where the bank employees parked. He hadn't wanted anyone to see his loaner truck and wonder what he was doing here, and Sadie had probably been thinking the same way. A tall hedge and a Dumpster shielded them from just about all angles. Good. He wanted her alone for a while.

Standing between his truck and her gray Toyota, her compliant smile died. "I told you I'd handle this on my own," she snapped.

"Since when do I take orders from you?"

Her eyes widened. Apparently she wasn't accustomed to arguments. She laid down the law, and that was that.

"This is my problem, not yours," she insisted.

Maybe it was time for Sadie to learn that he didn't roll over easily. "Well, it very quickly became my problem, wouldn't you say?"

Sadie looked tempting, with the sweater molded to her breasts and the skirt teasing him with a glimpse of her long legs. Too bad she was fearless in every area of her life but the personal.

"I'll handle it," she said.

"Do what you've gotta do. I'll do the same."

"Damn it, Truman!" She took a step toward him, a step that brought her very, very close. "Stay out of my way!"

He grabbed her arm, took a well-calculated step, and pressed her against the driver's-side door of his truck. A simple move, and they were caught between his borrowed pickup and her car, chest to chest and thigh to thigh. There was no one in the back parking lot at the moment. No one was likely to come out here until the bank employees started breaking for lunch. Truman pressed his body to Sadie's and held her in place. She didn't fight him; she didn't so much as tell him to back off.

"Stay out of your way," he repeated.

"Yes," she said breathlessly.

"Maybe I should go sit in your aunt's café and order coffee and just wait there and twiddle my thumbs until you've solved Garth's crime spree on your own."

She locked her eyes to his and licked her lips. Her heart was beating so hard he could feel it; her cheeks flushed and her dark eyes danced. And damned if he wasn't tempted to take her here and now.

"Sounds like a good plan to me," she said, probably not nearly as toughly and heartlessly as she'd intended.

He slipped his hand beneath her skirt and raked his palm up her bare inner thigh. She didn't tell him to stop. More importantly, she didn't look as if she wanted him to stop. "We can work together or we can work separately," he said, "but I'm not going to sit around and twiddle my thumbs and wait for something to happen." He ran his palm down the other thigh, taking his time, enjoying the feel of her skin in his hand. "Where's the gun?"

"In the glove box. Did you think I'd walk into the bank with a loaded pistol strapped to my thigh?"

"I wouldn't put it past you." He checked her thighs

again, both of them, brushing his fingers along the smooth skin that trembled.

"It's, uh, nice of you to try to help and all, but I really don't need..." Sadie began.

Truman raked his thumb across the thin slip of silk between her thighs. "I know what you need, Sadie Mae. But that's not what we're talking about right now, is it?"

She shook her head slowly, and even though she very well could have...she didn't move. He watched her get completely lost and distracted and carried away by a well-placed stroke of his thumb.

"You're better off without me," she whispered.

"Don't I have a say in that decision?"

"No," she said with a telling tremor. "You don't."

He slipped one finger inside the panties and touched her. Sadie was hot and wet and trembling, and while she said with conviction that she didn't need him, she sure enough wanted him. He felt the wanting in her body and saw it in her eyes. He was close enough for her to know that she wasn't the only one affected, here. His arousal pressed against her hip.

He stroked her, and she closed her eyes. Her thighs parted slightly, making it easier for him to touch her. "It'll be safer for you..." she said half-heartedly.

"I don't care about safe."

"But everything you need...everything you want..." Breathless and quivering, she arched her body against his and laid her hands on his hips.

"I don't recall you asking me what I want. As for what I need..." He took her hand and guided it to the erection that strained his jeans.

"That just...it doesn't mean...I don't want you to..."

"I'm not going to turn my back on you, Sadie."

Her eyes snapped opened and she looked squarely at him, in that fearless way she had.

"We're in this together, whether you like it or not." He stroked her harder, and the fire in her eyes changed.

She rested her forehead on his shoulder. "I don't want to drag you down with me."

"I don't need a woman to protect me."

"I know that," she whispered.

"Do you? Really?"

He shoved the narrow slip of silk aside and thrust one finger into her, then another. Sadie came quickly, clenching around his fingers and stifling a cry by catching it in her throat. Her body shook, and he wrapped an arm around her to hold her up. Damned if she didn't feel like she was about to drop to the ground, boneless and quivering.

She lifted her head slowly. Her eyes drifted open and she stared at him, unafraid and unashamed. Her dark eyes were so deep, he could easily get lost in them.

"You don't play fair," she accused.

"I play to win."

Her face was flushed, her eyes glazed. She had looked at him this way Friday night and Saturday morning, well-loved and sated and intoxicated. "Do you believe me when I tell you that I only want what's best for you?"

"Yeah. That doesn't mean I think you know what's best for me."

She leaned into him and let her body rest against his. "Even if I tell you to go away, you're going to keep investigating the murders, aren't you?"

"Yep."

"You're not going to give up."

"Never."

Sadie lifted her face and looked into his eyes, and he saw something new in her. Surrender.

"In that case, we might as well do this thing together."

This section of the park by Miranda Lake, a short walk from the parking spot where she and Truman had slept Tuesday night, was thickly wooded. Hikers occasionally came through on the weekends or during the summer, but it wasn't as heavily traveled as the walking trails or the docks. It was usually a pretty place, especially in the autumn when the leaves had turned, but today it had taken on a sinister and disquieting air.

"Davenport was the most recent murder," Sadie argued. "It makes sense to start with him."

Truman disagreed. "Everything goes back to Hearn. We have to consider the possibility that Davenport was only killed in order to point another finger at you."

The crime scene where Jason's body had been found was cordoned off and guarded by a sheriff's deputy and someone—not Evans—from the ABI, so she and Truman couldn't get any closer. Not that they needed to. Someone had called Davenport, lured him out here and beaten him to death. And—oh yeah—they had pretended to be her.

"Well, we're here now," she said reasonably. "Let's just deal with one thing at a time. You know everyone around here. Who hated Jason enough to kill him?"

"He annoyed a lot of people," Truman said. "Killing mad? I can't think of one."

"We know it was a woman."

"Or a man who can impersonate a woman's voice or has a woman working with him."

"You're not helping."

She had to keep Truman busy with Davenport's murder. Lillian would be crushed if word got out that she'd been Aidan Hearn's mistress up until a few months ago. If they got to a point where Truman had to be told, she'd tell him. Until then she was going to steer him elsewhere.

"Maybe someone was hoping the value of their wooden fish would go up if he was dead," Sadie offered dryly.

Truman snorted. He'd seen Jason's "artwork."

Her body still trembled, even though it had been hours since Truman had slipped his hand under her skirt and all but blown the top off her head. Instead of being satisfied, she wanted more. Tonight, when everything was done, would she be able to say goodnight at the door? Would she be smart enough to remind herself that he was better off without her?

Sex was easy; anyone could do sex. It was Truman's assurance that he wasn't going away that made her light-headed, when she let herself think about it.

While they studied the crime scene from a distance he placed his hand at the small of her back, and every feminine alarm she had went off and up.

Shoot, she might as well pack her suitcase and move into his room, because she was not going to turn her back on him again.

"What about the friend he was with when the call came?"

"Bradley Johnson."

Sadie wrinkled her nose. "I remember him from high school." His father had spent more time in jail than out, and his mother had been married three or four times, with numerous boyfriends in between. Bradley had never been quite right. "He's the witness? They're taking his word over mine? I'm insulted all over again."

"I don't blame you."

"Will he talk to us, do you think?"

Truman glanced down at her, and he smiled. Lillian was right—there was fire in him, and it burned brighter now than it had when she'd first seen him, sitting in the booth drinking coffee and watching the sun come up.

"I think Bradley will talk to you," he said. "He had a huge crush on you, back in high school."

"He did?"

Truman nodded.

"Ewww."

They didn't cross the crime-scene tape, of course, but there was nothing to stop them from walking through the rest of the park and doing their best to see what they could find. The deputy and the ABI investigator eyed them suspiciously from time to time, but there was nothing they could do to keep Sadie and Truman from walking the perimeter of the tape. When they'd arrived at the park a television cameraman from Birmingham and a couple of newspaper reporters had been on the scene, trying—without success—to get their questions answered. Earlier in the day there had been a few gawkers, but they had gone home, bored that there was nothing gruesome left to see.

Now she and Truman were the only civilians prowling about.

Even from here, she could see the place where Davenport's body had fallen. The blood on fallen leaves and uneven ground had turned dark, but that was clearly visible, too.

"He was a jerk," she said softly.

"Yep."

"Back in high school, now...a real jerk."

"I won't argue with you on that one."

She grabbed Truman's hand and held on tight. It was nice—the warmth and the closeness and the way he threaded his fingers through hers. "I never actually slept with him, you know. He dumped me because I wouldn't, not because I did. Again, a complete jerk. But he didn't deserve to die like this."

"No one does."

"We can't let the killer get away with this." She wasn't a do-gooder, she wasn't a crusader. She was good at her job and she was well-paid, but it was a job, not a calling.

But two people in Garth were dead, and if she knew nothing else she knew that it shouldn't have happened here.

Truman lifted her hand and kissed it. "We won't."

"I don't think I should be talking to you two," Bradley said with a shake of his head.

Sadie batted her lashes, and Truman almost laughed. He had never seen her play the damsel in distress. She did it well. The red sweater that hugged her curves didn't hurt matters any.

"I just don't know where else to turn," she said softly, turning up her Southern accent to a new level. "Why, some people actually think I called Jason to...to lure him out, and then I killed him. What am I to do?"

Bradley backed up and invited them into his trailer, which was located on an isolated lot not far from the park where Jason's body had been found. The rusting trailer was surrounded by pine trees and untended brush and the occasional squirrel.

"Maybe you'd better come on in and sit down," Bradley said, his eyes dropping down very briefly to study and appreciate Sadie's chest.

Sadie gave him a smile. "Thank you *so* much. I do feel like I need to sit a spell."

Bradley moved a stack of newspapers and made a place for a distraught Sadie to sit on the orange and brown plaid sofa, and she lowered herself gracefully.

Like Jason, Bradley had let his hair grow long. Like Jason, he did not have a great head of hair for such a hairstyle. While his greasy locks were much paler than Jason's had been, they were just as thin and unkempt. Where Davenport had been chunky, Bradley had the thin, gaunt look of a drug user, though his eyes were clear and he didn't seem to be under the influence of anything illegal at the moment.

The poor guy was under the influence of Sadie. Bradley looked at the woman who was perched on his couch like she was an ice cream cone and it was a hot summer day. He plopped himself down in the vinyl chair that faced her. Truman remained standing, apparently forgotten.

She straightened her skirt, in a girlish and obviously flirtatious way. "Thank you for seeing us, Bradley. I just don't know where else to turn. I didn't call Jason Friday night, I swear. Whoever called, it must've been someone pretending to be me."

Or else Bradley was lying and he knew darn well

someone else had called. That was a possibility they weren't ready to throw at him.

"I suppose. I didn't actually hear her, except for real faint in the background, you know. I could kinda tell from the voice that it was a woman. Jason told me it was you and that you'd had a change of heart and wanted to meet him down by the lake to…you know."

No heart was involved, of that Truman was certain. Bradley was scum, and he didn't like the creep even looking at Sadie. He wanted to grab the man by his ratty collar, push him against the wall, and threaten to shoot him if he didn't tell the truth. But he didn't. For now he kept his mouth shut and stood back to watch Sadie work.

"I was sound asleep when that call was made," Sadie said softly. "I swear it. I would never, ever hurt a living soul."

Bradley's eyes cut to Truman, briefly. No doubt he had heard where Sadie had been sleeping. Just as well. Truman wanted everyone to know that Sadie had been claimed. By him. He was willing to give Sadie room to work, but if Bradley made one wrong move Truman was ready and willing to cut the sucker off at the knees.

"Who would want to frame me that way?" Sadie asked, wide-eyed and pretty and almost innocent.

"Coulda just been somebody who knew y'all had had a date that went bad."

Sadie raised a hand to her chest. "You mean, I might've been a convenient diversion? A…a patsy for someone who wanted Jason dead?"

Bradley nodded his head. "I'm afraid that could be the case."

Sadie said, with a completely straight face, "I still don't understand why anyone would want to murder a respected artist."

Bradley, who had one of the atrocious wooden fish sculptures hanging in his trailer—it was red and purple and yellow, and the eyes were oddly humanoid—apparently held the same opinion of Davenport's art that Sadie and Truman did. He curled his lip, momentarily. "Jason had a hard time paying the bills with his art, so on occasion he picked up odd jobs."

"What kinds of odd jobs?" Sadie asked.

"Oh, you know...he picked up work here and there, when he needed to. For a while he worked at the grocery store, but they wanted him to cut his hair so he quit."

"I certainly can't see a motive for murder there, Bradley."

The smitten man leaned forward slightly and lowered his voice. "Well, I really shouldn't say, but the truth of the matter is, Jason dabbled in illegal drugs, on occasion."

Dabbled. Made it sound like a hobby.

"Jason *Davenport?*" Sadie said, apparently horrified. *"Drugs?"*

"Hard to believe, I know." Bradley shook his head. "I told Jason all along, I just don't cotton to that sort of business."

Yeah, Bradley was a real upstanding citizen.

"Do you think one of Jason's drug associates murdered him?" Sadie asked, a hand held to her chest in—again—horror.

"I suppose it's possible." Bradley was so intent on impressing Sadie. How much would he tell before he realized he'd gone too far?

"Could you possibly give us the names of these horrible people?" Sadie asked. "I mean, I know you're not at all involved, but if you ever heard Jason mention their names…"

"Nope," Bradley snapped, and Truman saw something in the man shut down. "I never heard a name or a detail or anything." They'd gotten all they were going to get, for today, but Bradley maintained his interest in Sadie. "Would you like something cool to drink? You look a bit peaked."

Truman reached out his hand, and Sadie took it. "Come on, sweetheart. It's time to go."

She turned those dark eyes up to him, all innocence and soft amusement. "Whatever you say, honeybun."

Bradley stood as Sadie did. "I know y'all are just looking for the truth, but I'd be obliged if you'd keep my name out of it. If anybody realizes that I knew Jason was into drugs and such, I could be in a heap of trouble. I surely don't want to end up in his sorry shoes."

"I won't tell a soul how helpful you were," Sadie promised. She turned her face up to Truman and… heaven above…batted her lashes. "We'll keep it our little secret, won't we, sugar lips?"

"Absolutely, darlin'."

Bradley locked the door behind his departing guests, and neither of them said a word until they'd climbed into the truck and Truman had started the engine. Then he turned to Sadie.

"Sugar lips?"

She wore a wide grin. A grin that told him she liked this sort of thing. The playacting, the danger…the rush. "Don't let it go to your head."

She was teasing, but he was deadly serious. "You've done that before, haven't you?"

"Done what?"

"Pretended to be someone you're not to get what you want. Batted your eyelashes at a man to get him to tell you something he shouldn't." *Called your backup sugar lips.*

"A few times. Believe it or not, a man will very often let a secret slip to a woman when he's completely shut down to a man. A smile, a flutter of lashes, maybe a heaving bosom or two…"

"I don't like it," Truman said as he pulled onto the gravel drive that would take them back to the road.

"What do you mean, you don't like it?" Her smile was wide, and there was a touch of laughter in her voice.

He didn't feel much like laughing. There were so many things about the picture Sadie painted that he didn't like. How was a man supposed to protect a woman who didn't want to be protected? "It's not safe."

After a moment she answered, deadly serious. "I don't have a safe job, Truman. You know that."

His hands gripped the steering wheel. "I know that very well. That doesn't mean I have to…"

His sentence was interrupted by a loud noise and the shattering of the truck's windshield. He swerved off the gravel road, and Sadie reached beneath her skirt and came up with a pistol in her hand.

"Son of a *bitch*," she said softly. "Now they're shooting at us."

Chapter 11

The official take on the shooting was that a hunter had been off his mark. Way, way off his mark. The bullet in the seat of Truman's borrowed truck came from a rifle, and it had missed both of them by mere inches.

It had been an exciting weekend all the way around. On Sunday, a fisherman had found Conrad Hudson's wallet and favorite baseball cap—both of them soaked and muddy—near an isolated launch used by local fishermen. Evans was going to arrange for the lake to be dragged, no small feat, since Miranda Lake was a good-sized body of water.

A gardening glove that appeared to be a match to the one found in Truman's pickup truck had been found near Jason Davenport's body. That fact was supposed to be confidential, but in a small town like Garth nothing stayed confidential very long. One of the deputies who knew and liked Truman called to give him a head's-up.

Evans looked at Sadie a little differently upon hearing the news about the close call. More thoughtfully, perhaps. But he apparently couldn't decide if the shooting was deliberate or a stunt she and Truman put together to make it look as though she was in danger. If he was smart, he would also be questioning the ease and convenience of finding those gloves that pointed to Sadie. She was smarter than that, and while he might not know whether or not she was capable of murder, he must certainly realize that she wasn't stupid.

Sadie knew one thing for sure. It was no longer safe for her to live with Lillian and Jennifer. What if the next time a bullet was fired at the apartment over the motel office? Or into the café when it was filled with customers? She couldn't stay in Truman's room, either. She didn't want to make him a target. It appeared that at this point everyone who came within spitting distance of her was in danger.

"They're keeping both trucks, but I have my cabin back." Truman jangled the keys at Sadie as he climbed into the passenger seat of her Toyota.

"Good," she said lightly as she sat behind the wheel. "You can go home."

"You're coming with me."

Her heart lurched, just a little. She wanted to do just that, more than anything. "That's not a good idea. I need to rent a house, or something, just for a few days. I don't mind being on my own," she said too quickly, "and I'm sure that arrangement would be safer for everyone."

Truman reached across and cupped the back of her

head, then pulled her slightly toward him. She loved the
way his hand felt on her head, the way his eyes softened
and flashed and hinted at the fire within.

"Let's get this over with once and for all, sugar lips,"
he said in a terse voice. "I don't care what you want, I'm
sticking to you like glue until this is over. I'm not going
away, I'm not burying my head in the sand, I'm not running off just because things have gotten a little hairy.
Got it?"

Her voice was small and oddly relieved when she answered, "Got it."

"You don't decide what's best for me, you don't
worry about what's safest for me, you don't try to push
me away. Cut it out."

"Okay."

"You're not doing this alone."

Sadie didn't mean to cry. She never cried! But tears
slipped down her cheeks, not because she was scared or
angry, but because for the first time in her life she really and truly felt that she was not alone.

"Don't cry." Truman wiped away her tears with a
gentle hand. "I'll take you home and I'll feed you, and
then I'll get you naked and make you forget what a terrible day it's been."

She managed a small smile. "It hasn't all been terrible."

"No, it hasn't."

Sadie had been shot at before. A single off-the-mark
bullet wouldn't bring tears to her eyes. She'd been in
trouble before. More than once. A sticky situation she
knew she'd eventually work her way out of would certainly not make her cry.

It was Truman, she knew that. He was more than a

friend, he was more than a lover, he was more than good back-up.

"I'm glad you're here." She leaned in and kissed him, hungry for that simple touch and the warmth that spread through her body.

"Me, too," he said, his lips soft against hers.

She let him kiss her, for a moment, and then she pulled slightly away. "How can you say that? I'm a walking disaster area. Two, possibly three people are dead. Two trucks, both of them yours, have been impounded. Last time I talked to Aunt Lillian, she was in tears." She didn't tell him why. Not yet. Like it or not, she was going to have to tell him soon. "I wanted to help Kathy, and instead I pushed too hard and drove her away. People are talking, and I really don't care what they say about me, but damn it, I do care what they say about you. Face it, Truman, since I've come home everything I've touched has turned to crap."

"Not everything," he said, his voice husky and promising.

After a quick trip to the motel in order to pack her clothes, Sadie said goodbye to Lillian and Jennifer. She didn't tell them that she'd been shot at—though they were bound to hear about the incident sooner or later—or explain that she needed to stay away from her family so none of the danger she had found here would touch them. If she'd been leaving with anyone other than Truman, Lillian probably would've tied Sadie down to keep her at the motel.

But Lillian liked Truman. More, she liked the idea of Truman and Sadie together.

Truman did everything he'd promised. Confiscating her car keys—an entirely macho move she actually let him get away with—he took her home. He fed her. He ran a warm bath and stripped off her clothes and when she was settled in the big bathtub he joined her in the water.

How quickly she had gotten accustomed to this. Truman's body against hers, his hands on her skin, the bone-deep feeling that she wasn't alone anymore. She leaned against his chest, and his arms wrapped loosely around her.

It was nice. All of it. The touching, the sense of belonging, the down-deep sense of home she'd felt since walking into this cabin. No, the sense of home that had scared her since she'd first laid eyes on Truman's face.

"Tell me what you want," she whispered. It was easiest to ask this way, when she could feel him but could not see his face.

His hands skimmed down her body and came to rest between her thighs. Large and calloused and very talented, they began to caress and arouse. "You know what I want."

She laughed. "No, that's not what I mean."

"No?"

"I'm trying to have a serious conversation here, and you're distracting me." He stroked a bit harder and her body responded in a way he could not mistake. She lurched a little and her breath caught in her throat. "Not what do you want now, right this minute, but...what do you want from your life?"

His hands came back up to caress her wet, soapy breasts. "That does sound like a serious question."

"It is. I think I know, but..." What if she was wrong?

It was a moment before Truman answered. "I don't think about what I want much anymore."

"Why not?"

Again there was a pause, as if he were carefully considering his answer. "Because when I blew out my knee I discovered that plans don't mean anything. You have to take life as it comes and make the best of it."

"Very philosophical of you, McCain."

"Realistic," he said, and then he rested his mouth on her shoulder. The lips moved, very gently. His tongue tasted and teased.

His hands slipped down to her belly, and rested there. "What about you? What do you want?"

"I don't know," she whispered.

"You must want something."

A shudder worked down her spine as the truth hit her. "No, I don't want anything, not anymore." She'd been hiding in her work, afraid even to consider what might be waiting for her down the line. Did she expect to be working for Benning when she was fifty? Sixty? Did she even plan, deep in her heart, that she'd live that long? "I don't have any plans at all."

"Maybe we can work on that."

"Maybe."

One hand parted her thighs and touched her where she had already begun to throb for him. He stroked, and kissed the back of her neck, and trailed the tip of his tongue over her shoulder. This time she didn't tell him to stop; she didn't want him to stop.

What did she want? Simple. She wanted this. Truman and this cabin by the water and his hands and his laugh and the way he looked at her. She wanted to be able to tell him that she loved him, to know that she did love him, and she wanted to hear him say those words to her. She wanted not to be afraid to tell him what she felt. Her body arched up to meet his stroke. So close...

"No," she whispered as she moved away and turned to face him.

"No?" He leaned back in the tub, aroused and content and sexy as hell. "Again with the *no?*"

"Not without you. Not this time."

Truman reached for her and she slithered against his wet chest and kissed him, while she wrapped her legs around his hips. Her body wanted to join with his now, wanted to rise up and slide down and take him in fast and hard.

But she wasn't yet sure that she wanted babies named Garfield or Cleveland. She wasn't even sure that she'd ever make a decent mother.

She didn't know that she'd ever be the woman who could love a man enough—and trust that love enough—to look him in the eye and give herself over to him, with her heart and her soul as well as her body.

So she stroked Truman's arousal with the palm of her hand, and kissed him so deeply she forgot where and who she was. Their tongues danced and they swayed together so that water billowed over the edge and splashed on the floor. It would be so easy to take him into her body here and now...

They stood, stepped from the tub, and headed for the bed and the drawer where the condoms were stored. Water rolled off their bodies and onto the hardwood floor and the rug and each other, and when they fell onto the bed and Truman reached for the drawer Sadie laughed lightly and stroked him one more time.

Quickly sheathed and still dripping wet, Truman hovered over her. "What do you want, Sadie?"

This time she didn't hesitate to answer. "I want you."

"Don't you have any ice cream?" Sadie asked.

Truman laughed. "You already ate it all."

She closed the freezer, reached into the cabinet at the right of the fridge and grabbed a bag of cookies, and walked into the great room, where Truman sat on the couch half-dressed.

She was half-dressed, herself. His shirt was longer than some dresses she owned.

He waited on the sofa; she grabbed her notebook and pen off the counter and sat in a fat chair.

Truman lifted his eyebrows. "We're here to work, McCain," she said, popping a cookie into her mouth and poising her pen over the notebook. "We need a little distance."

He stretched out on the couch, long and hard and oh, beautiful. "You'd better come over here. I think best when I'm…"

"You do not," she interrupted before he could say more, laughing. "Cookie?" she offered him one, and when he sat up with a sigh she tossed it to him. He caught the cookie easily.

"Jason's drug connections," she said as she made a notation at the top of the page.

"Possible, but all we have is Bradley Johnson's word. There's not that much drug activity in this county. A couple of small meth labs, some kids caught with marijuana. That's it. Even if Jason was involved, where's the motive for murder?"

"Think Evans will follow up on it?"

"Yeah, I just don't think he'll find anything."

Sadie tapped her pen against the paper. "What about personal stuff? Surely Jason has an old girlfriend who would make a decent suspect."

"Not that I know of. Evans is looking into that, I'm sure."

Sadie tucked her legs beneath her and took another cookie from the bag. She drew a cartoony fish next to Jason's name. It didn't help.

"Hearn," Truman prompted. "It started with him."

Taking a deep breath, Sadie wrote Aidan Hearn half way down the page. "What about his wife? I hear she's…"

"She didn't do it," Truman said before Sadie could say more.

"How can you be so sure? And do you realize, Truman McCain, that you defended her much more quickly than you defended me when Evans showed up accusing me of murder?"

He remained calm. "She's afraid of being alone. It's the reason she didn't leave him years ago. Hearn treated her like dirt on the bottom of his shoe, and she stuck with him. Unless there's a powerful motive I know nothing about, she didn't do it."

"Fine, but I'm not taking her name off the list until we have better proof than your gut instinct."

"My gut instinct is pretty good, most days."

She glanced at Truman, and caught him smiling at her. "I imagine it is."

"My money is on the other woman."

Sadie's heart leapt. She was going to have to tell him, and now was apparently the time. "Until a number of months ago, my aunt Lillian was seeing Hearn," she said.

She waited for him to jump off the couch, horrified at the revelation. Instead he gave her a calm, cool, "Yeah, but we know she didn't do it."

Sadie's spine straightened and she leaned toward the couch. "You *knew*?"

"Yeah. It wasn't exactly common knowledge, but it wasn't quite the secret Miz Lillian and Hearn thought it to be, either. This is a small town, Sadie. Nothing goes completely unnoticed."

"Does Evans know?"

"Probably not."

She relaxed. "You didn't tell him."

"He didn't ask." Truman shrugged his shoulders. "Besides, it was over almost a year ago. We need to concentrate on who he might've been seeing now."

"Like bubblehead Rhea."

"Yep."

Sadie carefully wrote "Rhea" on the page. Beside it, she drew a garishly high-heeled shoe and a fat pair of lips.

"Does Jen know?" she asked softly, her gaze on the paper.

"I don't know. I don't think so."

If Jen had found out about the affair, even well after the fact, would she have reacted violently? She couldn't bring herself to write her cousin's name on the page.

Truman asked for another cookie, and Sadie tossed it to him. "Either a woman he was involved with killed him," he said, "or he was involved in something we don't know about, or a serial killer coming through town just happened to pick on him."

Sadie's head popped up.

"I was just kidding about that last one."

"I didn't even think…"

Something about the expression on her face or the tone of her voice made Truman sit straighter and take notice. "Sadie? What is it?"

"Kathy."

"The waitress?"

Sadie set her notebook aside. "She said she was abused by her stepfather. If that's true, and from the way she told the story I believe it is, then she could very well have a serious mental problem, especially where older men are concerned."

"Hearn picks her up or they know one another some-how. She goes to his room, he makes a move, she kills him, either in cold blood or flashing back to what happened to her in the past."

Sadie sat back and drew in her legs. "Yeah. But that doesn't account for Jason or the missing Conrad. Un-less they somehow both threatened her. I just don't know. And why would she go to so much trouble to pin the murder on me?" She'd tried to befriend the girl, she'd done her best to help. "I just wanted to help her."

"No good deed goes unpunished, or so they say," Truman reached for the phone on the end table. "Given Kathy's past and her sudden disappearance, I think Evans might want to hear this tonight."

Sadie nodded and wrapped her arms around herself, suddenly cold. Logic or not, she couldn't see Kathy

Carson—or whoever she was—killing anyone…but then, she'd already confessed to one murder—that of her stepfather. Was she replaying that night? Killing men who touched her again and again.

"Yeah. I don't think he'd appreciate it if we waited until morning."

The earlier phone conversation with Evans—where he'd shared Sadie's suspicions about the girl who'd worked at the motel a few days and then disappeared—stayed on Truman's mind long into the night, but that wasn't what kept him awake. One way or another, the murder would be solved. Sadie would be cleared, and all the talk she worried about would died down. Some things wouldn't go away so easily.

A tumble or two with Sadie was one thing, but he had a feeling this relationship was turning into something more.

Relationship. Scary word for a man who had decided years ago that in the long run, women simply weren't worth the trouble.

He hadn't been serious about a woman since his divorce. It was easier that way. Sex was available without the forever after, and that was all he wanted or needed. He had even avoided anything resembling a regular sexual relationship, because he didn't want any woman thinking he could give more than he was willing to offer.

Which wasn't much.

Whenever anyone asked, he told people that Diana hadn't been fond of the small-town life, that she wanted the money and fame that came with being married to a star quarterback. That's what he'd told Sadie, when she'd asked. That's what he'd told everyone.

But the truth of the matter was, his marriage had begun falling apart long before the tackle that had ruined his knee and ended his career. Diana had never been happy. She'd always wanted more. More attention, more money. More men.

He'd been such a putz. Until he'd been confronted with the truth with his own eyes, he'd actually believed that his wife loved him.

Casual relationships that didn't last were fine, but he'd given up on anything more a long time ago, and until now he had never considered taking that chance again. Sadie made him think about taking that chance, and he wasn't sure he would thank her for that, when this was all over.

Something about the way they held on to one another even in sleep was terrifyingly hopeful.

He knew Sadie didn't want to stay here, and he wasn't sure he could leave for her. This cabin was his safety net. His place to hide. That's why he was awake at three in the morning, instead of sleeping soundly with this woman's body wrapped around his. Sadie had left the bathroom light on, since she was still unfamiliar with the layout of the room, and while what light made its way into the bedroom wasn't much, it was enough for him to see Sadie sleeping beside him.

He hadn't thought her beautiful in high school when she'd had that crush on him. He'd thought her pretty enough, and interesting, and different, but as a girl there had been a touch of awkwardness in her.

There was no awkwardness in her now, and she was beautiful.

While he watched she turned to face him, her eyes fluttered, and she reached across to rake her hand over his chest.

"You should be sleeping," she whispered, her voice smoky with sleep.

"So should you."

"I was. I was sleeping so good. And then I wake up and find you all the way over there on the other side of the bed."

"I didn't want to bother you."

She scooted closer and laid her head on his shoulder. "Restless?"

"I guess so."

"Me, too."

She sounded more awake, now, and the hand at his chest that slipped lower was definitely alert.

He rolled onto his side to face her, and for a while they just touched, as if they were just now learning one another's anatomy. Her curves; his contours. There was no rush in the way they stroked and aroused, no haste in the sighs or the way their bodies inched closer and closer until Sadie's leg was cocked over his hip and her mouth raked across his throat.

Sadie rolled him onto his back and straddled his hips, rising up above him like a queen of the night or the woman of his dreams. Dark curls wild, breasts full and soft, waist curving into perfect hips... And he was so close to being inside her again.

She reached for the bedside drawer, opened it, and grabbed a condom. While she ripped open the foil package, he placed his hands on her waist and said, "Have you ever thought about taking the pill?"

She grinned. "Impatient?"

"Yes."

She tossed the foil wrapper to the floor, but when he tried to take the condom from her she slipped out of the way and held it out of his reach. "I think I'll do the honors this time."

"Fine by me."

Sadie sheathed him, much more slowly than he could have done himself, but then she was having fun with the job. Her hands brushed against him, and she studied her work with dark and intense eyes, that half smile never leaving her face.

Chore done, she once again moved to straddle him, with the head of his erection barely touching her. She guided him into her body, slowly. Again she moved without haste, though there was now anticipation in her eyes. Truman watched their bodies join, watched them come together. Sadie was pale perfection, all woman and softness and beauty. He was tough and scarred and tanned from days spent by the lake, and even in the near-dark the difference was startling.

He was a little old and jaded to be awed by the fact that men and women are so very different, but at the moment that thought grabbed his mind and held on.

Sadie rose and fell slowly, her rhythm almost languid. She didn't thrust herself down to take all of him in, but teased them both with shallow strokes. They had all night for this, and she knew it and planned to take full advantage. Still, she wouldn't remain mellow for much longer, not if she felt anything like he did.

Sadie enjoyed being in control. Even now. Especially now. He let her set the pace, and when she looked at him with those dreamy eyes he cupped one breast and teased the nipple. Her entire body reacted. No, she wouldn't remain serene for much longer.

And she didn't. Her movements gradually grew harder and faster. Her breath came in a different way, shallow and bordering on frantic. She quivered around him, tight and hot, on the edge of climax.

He grabbed Sadie's waist in his hands and shifted his hips to plunge deeper. She cried out as she convulsed and quivered around him, her body lurched and grabbed him. His own climax came with hers, intense and complete.

Blinded by sex, he had the fleeting and frightening thought that he could love this woman forever, if she'd let him.

She collapsed atop him, warm and soft and slack, and made a noise of pure contentment into his shoulder. "I didn't know it was possible to feel this good," she said, her voice husky.

"The pill," he said again. He wanted to be inside her without anything between them. He didn't want to have to stop what they were doing to make sure there was no little Carter popping up to say hello in nine months or so. In the tub, in the middle of the night…wherever and whenever.

Sadie lifted up her head and looked down at him. Her cheeks were flushed, her hair was wilder than before. Her eyes had taken on a dreamy cast, and her lips were more full and sensual than he remembered. She looked like a woman who had been well-loved and didn't mind letting it show.

"It takes thirty days for the pill to be effective, you know," she said softly.

"No, I didn't know."

She didn't say anything else, and neither did he. They both realized it was very unlikely that they'd be together thirty days from now.

Chapter 12

"I can't, really…" Sadie said into the phone, not for the first time.

Lillian refused to listen. "Mary Beth is sick, Jennifer is taking care of the motel on her own, and the place is packed."

"But…"

"Your uniform is on your bed, freshly washed and ready to go," Lillian said crisply. "Please, Sadie Mae, I…"

"Okay," Sadie said quickly. "I'll be there as quick as I can."

It was now common knowledge that someone had taken a shot at Truman and Sadie, but everyone—Lillian included—had come to the same conclusion as the sheriff. It had been a hunter's wild shot, and nothing more. Given the limited list of suspects she and Truman had come up with last night, even Sadie had begun to think that might be the case.

But she wasn't sure. She hung up the phone and turned to Truman, who sat half-dressed at the kitchen table eating scrambled eggs and sipping coffee. He smiled at her and her entire body reacted. Heaven help her, she could get used to this.

"I have to go to the café for a while."

His eyebrows lifted slightly. "Is that a good idea?"

She sighed as she walked toward the bedroom to get dressed. "Probably not, but Lillian is insisting that she needs me, and damned if I can make myself tell her no when she calls me Sadie Mae."

In the bedroom she brushed out her hair and started grabbing things from her suitcase. "Mary Beth is sick again," she called. "I need to get that girl some vitamins or something."

Truman's response came from very close. He walked into the bedroom and headed for his closet. "She's pregnant."

Sadie spun around, a wave of horror whipping through her. "Again? Is there something in the water around here? That's two, count 'em, two employees coming up pregnant in a matter of months."

A very laid-back Truman whipped a green shirt off a hanger and grabbed a clean pair of jeans off a built-in rack. "I don't know the particulars."

Sadie dressed quickly. "I'm going to have to find someone else to work for Aunt Lillian. Someone reliable." Maybe someone past menopause, so maternity leave wouldn't even be a possibility.

"You'll find someone. Or else you can take over the

café yourself," Truman suggested. "I can't see Jennifer doing it, and Lillian isn't going to want to run the place by herself forever. She's not getting any younger."

"Oh, no," Sadie said with a shake of her head. "Lillian hàs plenty of good years left in her, and besides…I can't…I'm just not…" The words stuck in her throat.

"You're not sticking around that long, is that it?"

She turned to face Truman. He was dressed, and the happiness that had been so evident on his face all morning was gone. "You know I'm not," she said in a lowered voice. "You don't have to go to the café with me," she said as she headed for the door. "I'm sure I'll be fine."

He followed her down the short hallway. "Remember what I said yesterday about sticking to you like glue?"

"Yeah."

"Still stands."

"Yeah, but…"

"Besides," he said as he took the keys from her. "I'm not sitting around here with no vehicle."

She had often experienced that same fear; the terror of being stuck somewhere without any mode of escape.

He leaned down and kissed her. Not a deep kiss that would lead to more, but a sweet, intimate kiss that rocked her to her toes.

She could definitely get used to this.

Truman took a booth in the corner and sat with his back to the wall. He could see Sadie and the parking lot beyond the wide window and every customer in the place.

She refilled his coffee cup often and smiled at him when no one was looking. Not that everyone in town didn't know they were involved. Garth was the stereotypical small town, where everyone knew everyone else's business.

Usually. There were always secrets that managed to be kept. Apparently Hearn had had plenty of secrets and so had Davenport. If it had been just Hearn who'd been murdered, he might put his money on a spurned woman. But who would go to so much trouble to eliminate a witness and frame Sadie? That alone hinted at something bigger than a woman with a broken heart.

The lunch rush was almost over—there was less than half an hour left until closing time—when the two cars pulled into the lot. Alabama tags, but not from this county. Two men in each car. Fishermen? Maybe, but there wasn't a boat-trailer hitch on either of the vehicles, and if they had fishing gear it had been broken down and stored in the trunk.

One of the men, a large fair-haired man, went into the motel office with a sense of purpose and haste. Lillian was manning the desk and Jennifer was cleaning a few rooms, while Sadie and Bowie kept the café afloat. Truman watched the door to the motel office, but he didn't have to wait more than two minutes before the man came marching out, signaling to the others. Car doors opened, and the other three men stepped out. All of them headed toward the café, unsmiling and determined.

Lillian poked her head out of the office to watch the men cross the parking lot, but she soon poked her head back inside, like a shy turtle.

The big blond led the way. He was followed by a tall man with long black hair and too many tattoos, a slender dark-haired guy who looked like he'd been rode hard and put up wet and a slick fella in an expensive suit.

They all looked like trouble.

The door opened, and Sadie lifted her head and watched the men walk in. Her face actually blanched.

The blond glared at her. "Care to explain to me why the ABI is asking so many damned questions about you?"

"Not particularly," she answered sheepishly.

Truman sat back and watched, relaxing a little since it seemed that Sadie knew these fellas.

The man in the suit looked her up and down and grinned. "Nice look for you, Harlow. Where's the gun?"

"Bite me, Santana."

The other two each took a seat at the bar. They searched the café, sizing up every customer in a matter of seconds and finding no immediate danger. The man with the shorter hair, his eyes stayed on Truman a few seconds longer than was necessary. He stared; Truman stared right back.

Too many people were talking at once, and even though Truman couldn't make out every word, he could hear enough. The men teased Sadie for wearing pink and for pouring coffee like a pro. The blond, who was larger and older than the other three, didn't tease the way the others did. He wanted to know what was going on in Garth that had the ABI asking questions about Sadie.

She kept trying to tell him that she could handle it.

The four of them—obviously men Sadie worked with—sat at the counter and drank coffee and ragged on her. There was an easy camaraderie, and Sadie was a part of it. Truman didn't want to wonder exactly how close she was to these men…but he did. He couldn't help it. The one in the suit, Sadie had called him Santana, was much too familiar with her.

Truman didn't like it.

Sadie glanced back at him once after her cohorts arrived, but she didn't wave him over or smile. He got the distinct feeling she'd like to keep him far, far away from the men she worked with. When she refilled the coffee cup sitting before the slender man who looked like he'd lived a rough life, she stared into his face too intensely. Even from here, Truman could see her reaction. Her hands jerked a little and began to tremble. She put the coffeepot down hard. A little too rough or not, he was the kind of guy some women went for. Dangerous and crude, rough around the edges, he surely wasn't Sadie's type.

Was he?

Again, Truman had to admit that he did not know the woman Sadie had become.

Sadie felt like someone had pulled the rug out from under her. Literally. Her heart lurched, her stomach flipped.

Oh, those eyes. Green and sad and beautiful...

"Cal, I need to talk to you," she said, turning and walking toward the kitchen. She heard as well as felt Santana rise from his seat. "Alone," she added.

She sent Bowie to the front to see to the job of refilling coffee and taking payment from customers, and when Cal walked into the kitchen to join her—alone, as she had asked—she prayed that maybe, just maybe, she was wrong.

"Do you still have that picture of Kelly in your wallet?"

"Sure," he reached for his back pocket. "A trucker recognized her picture and said she's working in a bar outside Raleigh, North Carolina, or was last week.

That's where Mangino and I are headed, once Benning is satisfied that you're not in serious trouble."

She was definitely in serious trouble, but not the type the guys were worried about.

Cal removed the old photo from his wallet and handed it to Sadie. The picture had been taken in the junior year of high school. She'd lost weight, lost her innocent smile, and dyed her hair, but it was her.

"Your sister's not in North Carolina," Sadie said softly.

"What do you mean…"

"She couldn't have been in Raleigh last week, because she was here."

"Here?" His voice turned sharp. "Are you sure?"

Sadie returned the photo to Cal, and he blindly slipped it into his wallet and the wallet into his back pocket.

"I knew she looked familiar, but I could never put my finger on what it was. She doesn't look much like this photo anymore, but Cal, she has your eyes. That's what I kept seeing and recognizing. The eyes…"

"How long has she been gone?" he asked, with the stoicism of a man who was accustomed to being disappointed.

"Since Saturday," Sadie said. Kathy—Kelly—could be anywhere by now. This had happened so many times, it was downright frustrating. They'd get a lead on Kelly's whereabouts, a sighting, but either it turned out to be another woman who bore a resemblance, or by the time they got there she was gone.

At least now they knew why Kelly was running. Sadie's heart twitched. No, *she* knew. Nobody else. She didn't want to tell Cal, heaven above, she didn't want to tell him. But what choice did she have?

"What are you two doing back there?" Benning bellowed.

"We'll be out in a minute!" she replied in kind. She wasn't going to deliver this news in front of a crowd.

"Cal, I talked to her."

There was a touch of hope in his eyes. "Is she okay?"

Sadie started to nod, but Cal was her friend. A good friend. She didn't want to lie to him. "Listen to me." She took his hand and squeezed it. "And don't say anything until I'm finished." If he interrupted her, she didn't think she could ever finish.

"Okay." He squeezed her hand, much as she had just done to him, as if he knew that what was coming would be bad.

"Your stepfather raped her," she said softly.

Tears immediately sprang to Cal's green eyes.

"When he tried it a second time, she hit him over the head with a cast-iron skillet, and she ran."

"That's my girl," he muttered, his voice shaking a little.

"She thinks she killed him."

Cal shook his head. "He had a heart attack a few days after she ran away. Son of a bitch, I should've killed him myself." He got a dangerous glint in his eyes, one Sadie recognized. "I should've been there. He should've suffered…"

"Focus, Cal," Sadie said calmly. "Focus on Kelly and getting her back."

He nodded, but it wasn't easy for him to bury his outrage.

"She thinks you're dead and the cops are looking for her so they can charge her with murder."

"But…"

"I know it doesn't make any sense," Sadie interrupted. "But remember that Kelly was a kid when she ran."

A kid, violated and scared and on the run.

Tears ran down Cal's cheeks. He'd been tortured, shot, stabbed… She didn't even want to contemplate all the terrible things that had happened to Quinn Calhoun. And he'd never cried.

He swiped a hand at the tears that wouldn't stop. "I swear, Harlow, if you tell Livvie or the guys that I boo-hooed like a baby, I'll have to shoot you."

"It's okay." She wrapped her arms around him and gave him a hug. He needed a hug, even though neither of them would ever admit such a thing. He held her tight, and rested his head on her shoulder while he let a few more tears fall.

"It's not fair," he said against her shoulder.

"I know." She raked her hands up and down his hard back.

"I should've been there. I never should've let that nasty, dirty old man lay a hand on my little sister."

"You didn't know…"

"It's my fault."

"No," she said. "It's not your fault."

He quit crying, but he still held on. He held on as if he was afraid he'd fall apart if he had to stand on his own. "You know, Livvie wants kids, sooner rather than later."

Sadie patted Cal's back, trying to comfort him. How was it possible to comfort a man like this one? "Sounds like fun."

He shook his head. "No. Not fun. Not fun at all. What if I can't protect my kids any better than I protected Kelly? What if we have a little girl, and I can't keep her close enough or safe enough or…" He choked on the words.

"You're going to make such a wonderful father, Cal."

"Yeah, well, I'm a lousy brother."

He lifted his head and stared down at her. She had never seen him look so devastated.

"You are not a lousy brother, not at all," she said gently. "You've done everything possible to find Kelly and bring her home."

He had regained his composure, and was approaching his normal self. "She keeps moving. A kid shouldn't be able to hide and blend in and keep us guessing for so long."

"You could, if you had to."

Cal didn't argue with her.

"She's on the run, Cal."

"And now I know for sure what she's running from. I always wondered if he…"

"Don't," she interrupted. "The past is past. We can't fix it. All we can do is go forward."

"You're right. I have to focus on finding her. That's all that matters. You've seen her. I could use you with me. It wouldn't kill Santana to work with Mangino again. They've worked together before."

Sadie shook her head. "I can't leave town at the moment."

"So I hear." He sounded only a little disappointed.

"But I can work with a sketch artist and come up with a drawing that will do you a lot more good than that old high-school photo."

He leaned down and gave her another hug. "You're the best, Harlow."

She hated to tell him the rest. He likely wouldn't think she was "the best" when he found out that she'd put Kelly on the ABI's list of murder suspects. She told him, and while he wasn't happy with the wrinkle in the situation, he didn't hold it against her, either.

The men she worked with were like the brothers she'd never had. She adored them all, even if they did sometimes get on her last nerve. Like brothers.

"You really are going to be a great father, Cal," she said, giving his back one last pat. "Now, go wash your face." She stepped away and pointed toward the hallway that led to the employees' rest room.

He didn't immediately leave. "As soon as this mess is cleared up, you call me and I'll come fetch you."

She gave him a reassuring smile. "You know I will."

Cal turned and walked away, and almost ran smack dab into Truman.

"Excuse me," the man...Cal, Sadie had called him... brushed past Truman, barely paying him any mind at all. Apparently his mind was spinning with the news that he was going to be a father.

Sadie smiled at Truman as if nothing had happened. He did not smile back.

He had always known Sadie didn't intend to stay here, but he had never come to grips with the fact that he was nothing more than a diversion. Somebody to screw while she waited for her boyfriend to show up.

Expendable.

"Bowie left. He said you could lock up."

Sadie nodded. "No problem. Just as well that he's gone, I guess." There was the oddest expression on her face. Was she going to tell him about Cal? Daddy Cal? "I dread this," she said as she walked toward him. "Really, really dread it."

Was she going to tell him here and now that she was pregnant? That the Neanderthal was her boyfriend? No, not a boyfriend. Sadie had outgrown *boyfriends* years ago, he imagined. She was a woman who took lovers, not a girl reaching for a fleeting emotional attachment.

Instead of confessing, Sadie took his hand and led him back into the dining area.

The big blond asked, "Where's Cal?"

"In the little boys' room," Sadie said.

"What's up?"

"He'll be here in a minute," she said, ignoring the direct question.

Sadie led Truman behind the counter, so that a long span of Formica separated them from the men she worked with. She took a deep breath and let it out slowly, as if preparing for something difficult.

"This is Major Benning," she said, nodding to the blond man. "My boss. He's actually a retired major, but *Mr.* Benning just doesn't seem right."

Sadie's boss offered a meaty hand over the counter. "Benning will do."

"Dante Mangino," she said, moving on to the next man. "Part Italian, part redneck. Don't let the long hair and the tats fool you. He's one of Benning's finest."

Mangino smiled widely and offered his hand as well. Cal returned from his visit to the rest room, com-

posed and apparently recovered from his emotional out-
burst. He took the stool between Mangino and Santana.

"Quinn Calhoun," Sadie said. "Cal to his friends.
He's a mercenary, a hothead, and new husband to a
woman who is really much too good for him." There
was a hint of friendly teasing in her voice.

As the others had, Cal offered his hand for a shake,
and Truman took it.

Already, he felt like a grade-A chump. Maybe Cal
was going to be a father, but Sadie wasn't the mother.
She wasn't Cal's lover, she was his friend. The hug had
been…comfort of some sort. What she'd dreaded was
introducing *him* to her cohorts. He already knew that she
was an intensely personal woman who didn't like sharing too much of herself. Introducing him to the men she
worked with was a huge step for her.

He'd been so quick to jump to the wrong conclusion.
Sadie wasn't Diana. In fact, no two women could be
more different.

"And this is Lucky Santana," Sadie said with a sigh.
"He's the closest thing I have to a partner. We all switch
up now and then, but Santana and I have worked together a lot."

Santana did not smile like Mangino, and he did not
offer his hand. Instead he said, "We know who we all
are now, except for him."

Sadie took another deep breath. "This is my friend,
Truman McCain."

For a long, strained moment, the entire café was eerily silent. No one said a word. Sadie didn't even breathe.

"I always knew you had a *friend* stashed somewhere,"
Mangino finally said with a widening of his grin.

Benning just nodded and gave a little grunt, already bored with the conversation.

And Lucky Santana stared at Truman with an expression that said, very clearly, "Hurt her and I'll ruin your other knee."

The way they were looking at him, it was clear Sadie didn't have much of a personal life. At least, not that she had made her colleagues aware of. These men were like family to her, he imagined.

The dreaded chore of introducing him to her coworkers done, Sadie started talking—in a very businesslike voice—about contacting a sketch artist they had used in the past. Then she scooted down the counter so that she stood directly before Cal.

"Do you want to tell them?" she asked softly.

He nodded once.

And behind the counter, where no one else could see, Sadie threaded her fingers through Truman's and held on tight.

Chapter 13

To Sadie's absolute horror, all four of the guys decided to stay in Garth overnight. Benning wanted to speak personally with Evans, and the others were overly curious. About the murders and about Truman. She wasn't sure which intrigued them most.

And since Cal now knew the Kelly-sighting in North Carolina had to be false, he wasn't in a hurry to do anything but get back to his wife, who was now teaching at a county elementary school near Benning's headquarters in south Alabama.

Sadie grudgingly put them all up at the Yellow Rose Motel. Jennifer absolutely drooled over Mangino, whose hair was not even in the same ballpark as Jason's or Bradley's. Mangino's long black hair was the envy of many a woman, and it actually looked good. Great, even. Drool-worthy. This was the look the other two men had been aiming for—and had missed much more widely than the bullet had missed her and Truman. Sadie was not surprised that her cousin honed in on the most outrageous of the four men; Jen could spot trouble from a mile away.

Before she headed back to the cabin with Truman, she gave Dante a word of warning. He was not to mess with her cousin. He was not to so much as look at Jen and flash that Mangino smile. No argument. No, it didn't matter that Jennifer was over twenty-one.

Sadie wasn't sure if she was doing her best to protect Jennifer from Dante or if it worked the other way around. In the romance department, they both had a reputation for being, well, fickle.

She checked the rearview mirror often to see if anyone was following, as Truman drove toward the cabin. Not that she'd actually see anyone behind them if one or more of the guys had decided to follow her home. They were good. They were the best.

It struck her like a thunderbolt when she realized that she'd very naturally thought of Truman's cabin as home. Not a home she wanted to escape from, not a home to which she felt an obligation. Heart and roots and belonging, all the things she'd been so sure she didn't want, waited at the end of this road, and the fact that she was happy to be going there was terrifying.

Truman was quiet, his attention on the road before him and on…something else. Something he didn't share. Was he shocked by his brief confrontation with the men she worked with? Did he just now realize what her life was like?

If that was the case, he obviously didn't care for it.

Not at all. His jaw was tense, his eyes hooded, his mouth too firm. Even the hands on the steering wheel were tight and strained. It didn't matter that she'd just formed an unnatural attachment for a small cabin by a pretty lake, and for the man who lived in it. She wasn't what he wanted or needed—and she'd known that all along.

The cabin was in sight at the end of the long driveway when she asked, "Are you going to tell me what's wrong?"

He didn't hesitate to answer. "I'm an idiot."

For getting involved with her, for leaving his job, for getting caught up in this very personal investigation that got him shot at and fired…there were a lot of possibilities wrapped in that curt response. "Care to be more specific?"

"No," he said as he parked her Toyota at the back of the cabin, near the kitchen door. "But I think I'm going to have to."

The day was turning cool. Autumn would soon be gone, and winter would arrive. Winter in Alabama was rarely what any northerner would call brutal, but when the tree limbs were bare and the wind whipped across the lake, the cold could cut to the bone.

It had been a long time since she'd felt that Miranda Lake chill. She'd been so sure that she wouldn't be here long enough this time to experience it again, but day by day—minute by minute—things were changing. *She* was changing. Something deep inside her wanted to be here when the winter wind whipped across the lake, and when the crocuses bloomed, and when summer came with its long days and hot nights.

Truman took her hand and led her around the cabin and down to the pier. He belonged here—in Garth, in this cabin, by this lake.

And she didn't.

As they stepped onto the wooden pier, he began to speak. "When I walked into the kitchen and you were telling Cal that he would make a great father, I thought, for a few minutes, that you and he were…"

He didn't finish the sentence, and still Sadie knew exactly what he meant. "Cal's married!" she protested. "Very happily, I'll have you know. And even if he wasn't, I don't mix business with pleasure." In the past several years, she hadn't mixed *anything* with pleasure. She'd been all about business.

"I know that," he said, his voice soft. "But when I saw him touching you I just…I almost lost it."

The cold weather affected Truman's knee; he limped a little more than usual as they made their way, hand in hand, to the end of the pier. Sadie wanted to stop here in the middle of the pier, drop down and wrap her arms around that leg, kiss the knee and make it all better, and tell Truman that he didn't have to worry, not about her. She was his and always would be.

But she couldn't make his knee better, certainly not with a kiss, and even if in her heart she felt like his…was she? Truly?

"Diana had a thing for sportscasters," he said, his eyes not on Sadie but on the lake that danced on the autumn wind. "That's the reason she didn't get the chance to bleed me dry when we got divorced."

"Stupid bitch," Sadie said in a soft voice.

Truman actually smiled a little. "You always did get right to the heart of the matter."

She wrapped her arm around his waist, and drank in the warmth of his body. Where other people were concerned, she was quick to get to the crux. But when it came to her own life, it was a different matter entirely.

Truman draped his arm over her shoulder. "After I got rid of her, I swore I'd never get married again. Actually, I swore I'd never get seriously involved again. Not worth the trouble. My mother is always trying to fix me up with one girl or another, and she's forever talking about more grandkids. But I decided when I came here that there wouldn't be a second Mrs. McCain, no little Carter or Lincoln."

"I understand," she said. More than he would ever know, she understood….

"You're changing my mind, Sadie Mae," he said into the wind, "and I'm not sure that I like it."

Her heart did a sick flip, and her stomach tried to crawl into her throat. Instinctively, she tried to pull away. "I'll go…"

Truman held her tight. "Don't run. I'm not so sure I *don't* like that idea, either."

He drew her in close and kissed her, and she kissed him back with everything she dared to give. The kiss was deep, arousing and…romantic. Yeah, she was definitely coming away from this homecoming fling with more than she'd ever bargained for.

Truman turned her toward the cabin, and, with his arm around her, led her toward home.

"Let's get inside. I feel like someone's watching us."

"I know what you mean. It's probably Mangino and Santana."

He made a sound that was somewhere between a snort and a hum. "What about the other two?"

"Cal is talking to his wife on the phone, and Benning is hunting down Evans."

"You sound sure."

"Pretty sure." She smiled. "If Evans hadn't been treating me like a serial killer, I might feel sorry for him."

At this moment it was definitely easier to make a joke than to tell Truman that she was falling in love with him, too.

Truman woke with a start. For a few moments all seemed to be as it should be. Sadie slept beside him, naked and warm. The clock ticked. It was just after five-thirty in the morning, too early to wake without cause.

And then he heard it again…the shuffling noise outside the cabin that had awakened him in the fist place.

He shook Sadie lightly. "Sadie, honey. Would those fellas you work with be sneaking around outside the cabin for any reason?"

"Of course not," she said sleepily. "Don't be silly. Why would they do that? Go back to…" The noise came again, and this time Sadie heard it, too. Her head popped up, and she was immediately alert.

Without a word Sadie rolled from the bed, pulled on his discarded T-shirt, and reached for her gun. Truman did the same, only he grabbed a pair of jeans and pulled them on. Sadie was faster than he was. She was headed out the bedroom door, weapon in hand, as he zipped his pants.

He could call 911, but by the time anyone got here whatever was about to happen would be over. But just in case…

He lifted the bedside phone, but there was no dial tone. Whoever was out there had cut the phone lines, which meant their visitor was more than a large animal or a curious friend.

"Where's your cell phone?" he asked as he slipped down the hall behind Sadie.

"In my purse." His white T-shirt hit her at mid-thigh, but she seemed not at all aware the vulnerable state of her dress. Her mind was on what was happening, not what she was wearing.

She'd dropped her purse on the couch, as they'd come in for the night. "The phone line's been cut. Call…"

"I don't get a signal out here," she said, whispering as she edged into the dark great room.

A shadow passed before the window that overlooked the lake.

Sadie turned her head slowly to look at him. She wasn't afraid. In fact, she was more in her element than when she'd been pouring coffee or serving up Lillian's Wednesday surprise. Or sleeping in his bed. This is who she was, what she had become.

Sadie nodded her head once toward the rear door, then signaled that she wanted him to go out the front door. They'd head the prowler off. Every masculine instinct called for him to protect his woman…but the truth of the matter was, Sadie didn't need much in the way of protection. She could more than hold her own.

She slipped out the back door; Truman exited by the front. The sky was gray with coming morning, and outside the cabin his nose was filled not with crisp morning air but the stench of gasoline. The SOB had obviously planned to burn the cabin down with him and Sadie sleeping in it. Coward.

He heard a noise on the west side of the cabin. A whisper, the sound of liquid hitting the ground and splashing onto the wood. Truman stayed close to the house, rounded the corner, and saw their prowler. He couldn't deny that he was surprised.

Rhea Powell, Hearn's assistant—and maybe his lover, according to Sadie—splashed gasoline along the ground around the cabin and even into the wood itself. She had dressed in black for the occasion, and had her hair pulled back in a casual ponytail.

Truman raised his gun and aimed it at Rhea. "Hold it."

The woman's head snapped around, and she was openly surprised to find that she'd been caught. An expression of fear crossed her face, but didn't last. After a moment, Rhea actually smiled.

"It would have been easier if you'd just stayed asleep, Deputy McCain," she said.

He heard a softly shuffling footstep behind him. Sadie had circled the house in the opposite direction and had taken the long way here.

When Truman heard the grating scuffle of a hard heel dragging across the rocky ground, he knew it wasn't Sadie. She'd been barefoot when she'd slipped out of the cabin. He spun, too late.

Conrad Hudson, the Yellow Rose Motel's missing desk clerk, popped Truman on the side of the head with a gun—Sadie's gun?—and kicked out at the bad knee. Truman crumpled, pain shot through his leg and his head, and everything went black.

Sadie reached for the knot on her head, but it was difficult, being that her wrists were tied together. Half awake and groggy, she gasped when a handful of cold water was splashed onto her face.

"Come on," Conrad said brusquely. "Wake up."

Sadie's eyes drifted open. The sky was a touch lighter than it had been when she'd been cold-cocked from behind. All her attention had been on the prowler sneaking around Truman's cabin. The second one had surprised her. Stupid! She never should've allowed him to sneak up on her.

"You crooked son of a bitch," she said as she struggled to sit up. He had dragged her all the way to the end of the dock, so that she sat not two feet from the edge. She glanced up. Conrad looked annoyed, and more than a little jumpy. Criminal mastermind he was not.

"I don't want to do this, I really don't. But you just haven't left us any choice."

Us?

"I wish I could just shoot you and dump you in the lake and get it over with, fast and easy," he said, shuffling his feet.

It gave Sadie a small amount of hope to know that Conrad didn't want to kill her. Maybe she could talk her way out of this. "That wouldn't be very smart," she said, her voice calm. Then again, Conrad had proven that he wasn't very smart. "You won't get away with it."

"I didn't want to hurt you. Damn it, Sadie." Conrad wiped at his forehead with his free hand, sweating even though it was quite chilly. "Why did you have to bring those goons to town? With all their questions and their snooping, they're going to ruin everything."

"You think they'll quit snooping if you shoot me?" she asked. "Think again." Her eyes shot to the cabin.

Where was Truman? Had he gotten away? Maybe gone for help?

No. If he was able he'd be here, odds or no odds. She knew that. Her stomach sank. What had they done to him?

Rhea Powell, Hearn's airhead secretary, stood by the front door of the cabin, waiting for something. She looked bored, standing there with all the weight on one leg and her head cocked to one side as if she were sitting in a bar, posing and trying to pick up a guy for the night. She waved her hands expressively at Conrad.

Sadie felt like an idiot. How many times had she played the airhead? Plenty. Everyone underestimated a woman who was only interested in her hair and her nails and her shoes.

"What do they know?" Conrad asked, turning his attention to Sadie once again.

"What does who know?" Sadie asked calmly.

"Those men at the motel," he said, his voice quick. "What did you tell them?"

"What difference does it make?"

"Rhea wants to know."

It was pretty clear Rhea was the brains in this two-man operation. "Rhea wants, Rhea wants," Sadie droned. "Did you kill Hearn for her?"

Conrad shook his head quickly. "We're not going to talk about that. I just want you to tell me what those men know."

Sadie ignored the question. "What about Jason? What did he do to get on Rhea's bad side?"

The way Conrad cut his eyes to the side and swallowed hard... He might not have killed Hearn, but he'd definitely had something to do with Jason's death.

"Did Rhea make you kill him just to make the cops come after me? Is that it?"

He didn't deny it. Bingo.

"And then you planted that bloody glove in Truman's truck, because you knew I was here that night."

"It was just to throw them off the scent, that's all," Conrad muttered.

"How many more people do you think Rhea's going to ask you to kill, Conrad?" Sadie asked in a soft voice. "Is there going to be an end to it? Are you really going to shoot me?"

"You're not going to get shot," Conrad said, his voice steadier than it had been a few minutes ago. Apparently he had made his decision, and she wasn't going to be able to talk him out of anything. "You're going to drown running away from the fire."

"What fire?"

He looked at Rhea once again and shrugged his shoulders, indicating that he wasn't getting the information she had asked for. The woman reached into the pocket of her tight black pants for something small. Sadie knew what Rhea held in her hand when she lit a match and tossed it at the cabin.

The fire caught quickly and spread, eating up the gasoline that had been poured around the building.

Home.

Sadie tried to jump up, but her ankles were tied with a rough length of rope, much as her wrists were. She almost fell, but caught herself just before pitching forward and landing on her face. On her knees, she watched the fire spread. Rhea stepped toward the pier and away from the heat of the fire.

"Where's Truman?" Sadie asked.

"Inside," Conrad said in a low voice. "Unconscious. He won't feel a thing, I promise."

Her heart started to pound, her breath caught in her throat. Not Truman. She didn't care what happened to her, but she couldn't bear it if anything happened to him just because he'd had the misfortune to get involved with her.

"Drag him out of there and I'll tell you anything you want to know," she offered. "I'll send the goons home. I'll confess to both murders. Just…get Truman out of there."

Conrad stepped closer to her. "It's too late for that. All you had to do was sit back and let the sheriff and the ABI do their work. There might not have been enough evidence to convict you, but as long as you were the prime suspect they didn't have any reason to look at me and Rhea."

"Why?" Sadie asked, her eyes on the fire.

"Money," Conrad answered. "Lots of it. Rhea's really good with computers and such. Now and then while Hearn was out of the office she just moved things around a bit. Not a lot, not at first, but it did add up after a while."

"She's a common thief," Sadie snapped.

"Not so common, if you ask me. She's been moving money around for years." He wrinkled his nose in distaste. "A few months ago Hearn figured out what she was up to. But instead of calling the cops, he demanded a cut and he made her sleep with him, even though she really wanted to be with me."

Yeah, make *her* out to be the victim. "She's a thief,

and Hearn was blackmailing her. Sounds to me like they deserved each other."

"No, you've got it all wrong. Rhea wanted to be with me, not him. She got tired of letting him put his hands on her, and last week he got rough with her and she had to defend herself. There's nothing wrong with that, is there?"

"You don't really believe that story, do you?" Sadie shouted. "She wasn't defending herself. I saw the body. The man was reclining in the bathtub and she cut his throat. More than once, Conrad. She butchered him!" Her eyes cut to the cabin. The fire continued to spread but it hadn't yet gotten out of control. "She's using you just like she used Hearn. Once you do her dirty work, how long do you think it'll be before she slits *your* throat?"

Conrad looked genuinely shocked at the concept. "Rhea wouldn't do that. She loves me."

"Women like that don't love anyone but themselves. And money, of course." Sadie kept her eyes on Rhea and the fire that now licked at the sides of the cabin. "What do you want to bet you have it all wrong?" she asked softly. "I'll bet Rhea was with Hearn because she liked it, and she killed him because she got tired of sharing her precious money. She wants it all for herself, Conrad. Where do you think that leaves you?"

"No, you're wrong. She loves me."

"You're the patsy, Conrad. The cops already think you're dead and resting at the bottom of the lake, so if she does away with you, who'll be any the wiser?" She looked him in the eye. "Let me go, and I'll help you. You don't need that tramp leading you around by the nose."

Conrad kicked Sadie in the side. "Don't talk about

Rhea that way." He pointed the pistol—her own freakin' pistol!—at her face. "We're running out of time. What do the goons know?"

Sadie made herself smile at him. "Everything, you sick SOB. They know everything." Maybe she couldn't save herself or Truman, but if these morons went after the Benning boys they wouldn't have a chance. It was small comfort...

The door to the cabin flew open, and Rhea let out a high-pitched scream. Face covered with a raised arm to shield himself from the thick smoke, Truman rushed out. It looked like he could barely walk at all, but he did manage to grab Rhea and rush them both away from the burning cabin.

Conrad was distracted by the commotion, no doubt worried about Rhea and what might happen to her. Sadie took the opportunity to rise swiftly and swing her bound hands up to knock the pistol out of his hands. The weapon landed on the pier and skittered away.

Truman pushed Rhea to the ground and started to run. Toward Sadie. He wasn't supposed to be able to run, even on a good day. But he did. Eyes on her face, Rhea and the burning cabin forgotten, he ran to her.

Unarmed, Conrad kicked at Sadie again. His boot found her belly, and she stumbled back. One step and she was almost steadied. The next step found air. For a moment she was suspended in midair, falling and breathless. Her attempt to catch herself on the edge of the pier failed. But she did manage to pitch herself forward. Just enough to bang her head on the edge of the weathered wood.

She landed in cold, wet darkness, disoriented and on the verge of passing out, and she sank like a stone.

Chapter 14

Sadie fell into the water, disappearing in a split second with a splash.

Her hands and feet were bound; she couldn't swim.

Truman ran, focusing on Conrad and ignoring the pain in his leg. He shouldn't be standing, much less running, but dropping or even slowing down now wasn't an option. Sadie was in the water, damn it.

Conrad reached for the gun Sadie had knocked out of his hand. It had gone sailing a good four or five feet, so he had to scurry to reach it. The man who had kicked Sadie into the lake fell to his knees and lunged for the weapon but Truman reached it first. He scooped up the pistol while Conrad's slender fingers were mere inches away.

The part-time desk clerk who had been missing for more than a week and presumed dead for much of that week was frightened and unarmed. His hands popped up and he shook his head in quick, jerky motions. "Don't shoot me. It was all her idea. I didn't want to kill Jason, I really didn't."

Truman's eyes darted to the rift in the water where Sadie had fallen. He kept expecting her head to pop up out of the lake for a gulp of air, but it didn't, and with every split second that passed he was achingly aware that she couldn't breathe.

"No need for this to get ugly," Conrad said, his eyes on the gun.

In the distance, sirens wailed. Someone had seen the smoke from the fire, and help was on the way. Fire department, the sheriff and his deputies, the volunteer EMTs. Maybe even Evans, if he figured out where the smoke was coming from.

The water went still. Now there wasn't even a ripple where Sadie had fallen.

Truman spun, took aim, and fired. Rhea dropped to the ground screaming, thinking he was shooting at her. But when the front tire on the car Conrad had parked near the far end of the drive popped, she straightened up and started in surprise. Conrad made a frantic move toward Truman and the gun, but Truman was ready for him. An elbow in the gut and a twist of the arm, and the man went sailing into the water.

Rhea turned and ran. Not toward the pier in order to help Conrad, but away from the scene.

Truman tossed the pistol into the lake—in case Conrad made it out of the water before he did—and then ran a few more steps, diving into the spot where Sadie had fallen.

Beneath the water he couldn't see anything. It was

too dark, too cold. Damn it, Sadie couldn't swim, but she should be able to kick her feet and float a little! The water was too murky for him to see much of anything, but rising to the surface without Sadie was unthinkable. He kept pushing downward, kicking his feet and reaching into the darkness, until he saw the dim light of something other than mucky darkness before him. Pale flesh. Dark hair floating. Sadie did wiggle, perhaps as much as she could given the way she was bound, but her movements were small and ineffectual and did nothing to push her up.

Truman reached out. His hand manacled Sadie's wrist and he started kicking, propelling them both to the surface. His head came up out of the water, and he took a deep breath that filled his lungs with cool air. Sadie had been down longer than him…just a couple of minutes, but when you can't breathe, a couple of minutes is a very long time. She, too, took a deep ragged breath as her head came up out of the lake.

He kept her head above water and paddled toward the ladder at the end of the pier.

The sirens were closer now…they were in his driveway. Conrad climbed out of the lake, dripping wet and shaking.

"Come on, Sadie," Truman said as he kicked and steered himself and the woman in his arms toward the pier ladder. He kept her chin, mouth and nose above water, as he inched toward safety. "Talk to me."

Instead of talking, she coughed raggedly and spat up some water. That done, she took another deep breath.

Conrad ran, but it was too late. Not only was his

front tire flat, he was now blocked by the arriving fire trucks and two patrol cars.

Truman reached the ladder. He wasn't sure he could climb it alone, much less get an obviously weakened Sadie up there. Bryce, who had been in the lead patrol car, was there to offer a hand, thank goodness. Together they got Sadie onto the pier, where she lay back and closed her eyes, and then Truman climbed the ladder himself, again with a hand from Bryce.

He sat beside Sadie, still catching his breath and trying to make his heart rate slow to a normal rhythm. His T-shirt, the white one Sadie had grabbed and pulled on as they'd left the bed, was soaked and all but transparent. He watched each breath she took with relief while he worked on the wet knots at her wrists.

"Blankets," he rasped, and Bryce turned and ran.

Behind Truman the cabin was going up in flames. He didn't even turn to look. The fire department was doing their best, but he knew everything had been lost.

No, not everything. Sadie was all right and so was he. At the moment nothing else mattered.

When her wrists were freed he worked on the rope at her ankles. The knots were wet, but came loose easier than he'd expected they would. Sadie didn't move. She lay there, silent and still, while he removed the ropes and tossed them aside.

"Open your eyes and talk to me," he commanded, his gaze riveted to Sadie's face.

For once, she obeyed his command. Her eyes drifted open and she looked at him. "I couldn't breathe," she rasped.

"I know."

Sitting on the pier, soaking wet and cold, he lifted Sadie and pulled her into his arms. She clung to him, shivering.

"I'm not dead," she said, sounding truly surprised.

"No, you're not."

"I thought, for a minute there…" She didn't dwell on what might've happened. A shiver worked through her body. "I'm cold."

He hauled her into his lap and ran his hands up and down her back, trying to generate a little warmth. Bryce came running back, a wool blanket fetched from the trunk of his patrol car gripped in one hand. Truman took the blanket and wrapped it around Sadie.

"Damn it," she whispered. "Did they get away?"

Truman glanced toward the house, where Sheriff Wilks had Rhea and Conrad well in hand. Rhea might've tried to run, but she hadn't gotten far. "No. They didn't get away."

Sadie sighed in relief, then she lifted her head slightly to watch the cabin burn. There was such a deep sadness in her eyes, he knew she hurt for what had been lost.

"I'm so sorry." Her voice was small. Almost child-like. "It's all my fault."

"No, it's their fault."

"Your cabin…"

"Can be rebuilt," he said before she could go further.

She rested her head against his chest, then took the ends of the blanket and wrapped it around him, so they were both cocooned in its warmth. Heat began to return to his skin.

Bryce stood over them, unsure about what to do. He wrung his hands. "The EMTs are on the way."

"Radio in and send them back," Truman insisted.

Bryce shook his head. "I can't do that."

"We don't need any EMTs," Sadie insisted. "We just need a few minutes to catch our breath. And maybe another blanket."

"I can handle that," Bryce said, happy to have a job once again.

When he was gone, Sadie lifted her head and looked Truman in the eye. "You ran."

"I did." He likely couldn't walk at the moment, but when it had counted, he'd done what he had to do.

"You saved my life."

"You'd do the same for me."

Bryce returned with the extra blanket. He wanted to move Sadie to a patrol car and wait for the EMTs there, but neither of them were willing to move at the moment. So Bryce stepped to the end of the pier and let them be for now. They sat on the pier wrapped in two wool blankets, hanging on to one another for dear life.

The fire department quickly got the flames under control. Maybe the cabin wouldn't be a complete loss, after all.

Sadie relaxed until she was limp against him, her arms wrapped around his waist and her body shivering, a little. She actually fell asleep, completely exhausted by the ordeal in the lake. As long as she was breathing, that's all that mattered.

Truman brushed a strand of hair out of her face. "I can replace the cabin," he said softly. "I can replace the building and everything in it, but I can't replace you. I love you, Sadie Mae," he added beneath his breath. "What am I going to do about that?"

Conrad was talking freely, much to Rhea's dismay. He tried to put a noble spin on it, but the truth was that Rhea had been sleeping with Hearn and giving him a cut of what she embezzled for months.

.She must've been planning the murder for a long while, because she'd been building her relationship with Conrad for all those months; since just a few weeks after she and Hearn became involved. Sadie didn't believe in coincidence, so it must've been a part of the plan.

Hearn always chose the nights when Conrad was on duty for their rendezvous. Maybe so he wouldn't have to see Lillian at the front desk, or so she wouldn't know who had taken her place. Rhea coaxed Conrad into keeping the secret of the affair to himself, and even slept with him a time or two in order to keep him on a string.

Women like Rhea gave an entire gender a bad name.

Rhea had known Conrad would be interviewed once Hearn's body was found, and she'd also known he was weak. It had been her idea that he disappear. It had also been her idea to kill Jason Davenport, when she heard about the fight he and Sadie had had at the Shamrock. But that time Conrad had done the dirty work. Rhea had done nothing more than make a phone call, pretending to be a contrite Sadie.

Standing in the motel parking lot, Sadie reassured all the guys she worked with that she was fine. Cal bought it, and so did Mangino. Even Benning seemed pretty much satisfied. After all, she'd been through worse and they all knew it.

Lucky Santana was not satisfied by her account of the morning's excitement. He glared at Truman as if it was *his* fault she'd been thrown in the lake, when all he'd done was save her life.

They had a nice, warm room waiting for them. Truman—knee bandaged tightly by the EMTs who had arrived just five minutes after Wilks had taken Conrad and Rhea away—didn't need to be climbing the stairs to her room above the motel office just yet, and she wasn't about to leave him alone.

All the guys, except for Lucky, left to pack their bags.

Sadie handed Truman the key to their room. "Go on in. I'll be right there."

He raised his eyebrows slightly, in silent question.

"I need to have a word with Santana."

He didn't like it, but he did unlock the door to their room and step inside.

Sadie wore pair of borrowed pants that were several sizes too large, a loaner of a T-shirt that all but swallowed her whole, and a blanket that kept the chill off. All she wanted was a long, hot shower, something to eat, and Truman.

She smiled up at Santana. "Quit glaring at me that way."

"You can't *swim*?" He sounded not only angry, but horrified. There was actually a spark of fire in his normally distant eyes.

"No, I can't. Is that why you're angry? Because I can't swim?"

"You never told me," he said more calmly.

"It never came up."

She knew, in a flash of instinct, that Santana's anger had nothing to do with her inability to swim or her oversight in telling him about the failing.

He knew she was leaving, even before she did.

"You work really well with Mangino and Cal," she said, "and I'll bet if Murphy ever gets any field time…"

"I'm not a freakin' baby-sitter, and I'm not looking forward to breaking in a new partner." He scowled. "Damn it, Harlow, you're the only woman I ever trusted to watch my back."

She slipped a hand out of the warmth of her blanket and touched his face. Perfectly clean-shaven, jaw hard and nostrils flaring, he was a sight. But she wasn't afraid, not even of Santana's anger.

"I love him," she whispered. "I really should *not* be telling you this before I even tell Truman, but…I love him so much." Her smile grew. "I waited a long time to find him."

Santana put his hand over hers and drew it away from his face. "Love is just lust wrapped up in a pretty package." He gave her a long-suffering sigh. "If you just needed someone to scratch your itch, all you had to do was ask."

Another woman might be insulted, and she couldn't deny that once upon a time the thought had crossed her mind. "It's not about that," she said, and then she smiled. "Well, not entirely."

Santana rolled his eyes.

"I love you like a brother, Lucky, I really do. But Truman is my forever."

He growled, a little. "Call me in six months, when the new of this relationship has cooled off, and we'll see what you think about *forever* then."

It was time to face Truman. She did love him, she did want forever. But she wasn't sure he'd feel the same way. Thanks to her he'd lost his job and his cabin had been burned to the ground. His knee was hurting, and there was no telling how long it would take to heal properly.

Santana saw the indecision in her eyes. "If McCain gives you any grief, I'll take care of him for you."

"No, you won't." She smiled one last time and slipped her hand from his.

There were no guarantees, there was no promise that would make Truman love her, now and forever. But if she didn't try...what would she have?

The door to their room was propped slightly open, and Truman sat on the side of the bed, waiting for her. He lifted his head when she walked into the room, and looked at her with a question in his blue eyes.

"I had to say goodbye to a friend," she said as she locked the deadbolt.

She dropped the blanket and walked to Truman, sitting beside him and wrapping her arms around his waist, all in one smooth move. His arms went around her, too, and they fell back onto the bed together.

It seemed like ages since they'd been alone, even though it had only been a few hours.

There was so much to be said, but for the moment it was easier just to hold on and take comfort in touch. She could undress Truman and herself, make love to him, and then…when they were hiding under the covers and sated and half-asleep…then she could tell him.

But that would be the coward's way out. "We need to talk," she said, trying to sit up.

Truman laughed hoarsely and held on to her as he fell back on the bed. They landed still entangled, bouncing lightly. "Then talk," he said, keeping his arms securely around her.

Sadie was more nervous than she'd been when she'd thought Conrad might shoot her. With good reason. Her life depended on what happened in the next few minutes.

"Ask me what I want."

"Now?" He cupped her breast and teased it.

"Now," she whispered.

He took a deep breath and closed his eyes, as if he dreaded the conversation to come. "What do you want, Sadie Mae?"

She scooted closer, as close as possible, and placed her face closer to his. "I want to help Cal find his sister."

That got a small, displeased grunt out of him. "That's kinda what I figured you were going to say."

But Sadie wasn't anywhere near finished.

"I want to be your soft place to fall," she added quickly. "Not just when I come back to town for a visit now and then, but…" She said the word that terrified and thrilled her. "Forever."

Truman's beautiful blue eyes opened, and he looked at her.

Sadie brushed aside a lock of soft brown hair that had fallen across his forehead. "I want to stand beside you at the next election, when you run for sheriff and kick Wilks's ass. I'll even leave my gun at home that day."

He smiled, a little. "You really think you can learn to leave the house unarmed now and then?"

"Yeah, I think I can. Unless, of course, I'm working a case." She slipped her leg through his, taking care with his bandaged knee. "You will need a lead investigator if you plan to bring the Sheriff's Department up to speed."

"I guess I will," Truman said with a half smile.

"I want to be there when you rebuild the cabin. I want to *help* you rebuild your home." Our home? Maybe. It all depended on where this conversation ended up. "We might want to make it a little bit larger, add a room or two onto the back, because one day I want a daughter named Reagan and a son named Grant or maybe Pierce."

Truman shifted his head to her throat and kissed her there. Once, twice.

Now came the tough part. "Most of all, more than anything, I want you to love me the way I love you."

She waited for him to say something. Anything. It was very much like drowning.

Truman rested his hand in her hair and lifted his head to look her in the eye. "I do love you."

Exhausted but deliriously happy they rested there, with her head on Truman's chest and his hand tangled in her hair and their legs entwined. She was so tired, and now that she'd taken the leap and told Truman how she felt, everything seemed good and fine. Her body felt heavy and tired, and it demanded rest. Her eyes drifted closed. Everything was going to be all right.

"We'll rebuild the cabin," Truman said, "and we'll add on a few rooms at the same time."

She smiled, and a new warmth shot through her. "Teach me to swim?" she said with a yawn.

The last words she heard before drifting into a deep sleep were, "Oh, yeah."

The clothes and shoes were borrowed but dry. His knee was tightly wrapped to keep it from giving out on him, but he was able to maneuver on his own. No crutches required. Truman stepped out of the hotel room, headed for the café and something to eat. Something to go. Sadie was ravenously hungry, and she wasn't ready to leave the bed. If he had his way, she'd stay there all day.

It was Wednesday, time once again for Aunt Lillian's Gelatin Surprise. Truman shuddered. Maybe Lillian would give in and make a plate of sandwiches, since it was for Sadie.

Great. All four of those Neanderthals Sadie worked with were hanging out in the parking lot, watching his door, waiting for him—or Sadie—to exit.

He took a step toward the café. They all walked toward him, like linebackers intent on bringing him down.

They met in the middle of the parking lot.

"We're getting married," Truman said without preamble. "Next week."

"Next week?" Benning shouted. The four of them stood between Truman and the café. "Sadie can't get married next week! We have work to do!"

"Sadie will work part-time for a while," Truman said calmly. He looked at Cal. "She really wants to help you find your sister." But if he had his way she'd be pregnant soon, and then she'd think twice about chasing around with a gun strapped to her thigh.

Maybe.

"Why are y'all still here?" he asked. "The excitement is over."

"We want to make sure Sadie's okay," Mangino said. "And besides, the sketch artist she asked for will be here in an hour or so."

"She told me about that."

Santana, who looked at Truman like he wanted to break something, said, "She's hungry, right?"

"Right."

"The woman eats like a horse," Santana said, unsmiling, "and when she comes down off an adrenaline high, you'd better be somewhere near a Dairy Queen."

He hated it that these men knew more about Sadie than he did.

No, not more. What they knew was different, and he had time to learn it all for himself. All the time in the world.

"Thanks for the tip." Truman glanced toward the café. The place was empty. Then again, it *was* Wednesday. "Let me buy y'all lunch," he said, clapping Santana on the shoulder.

Benning was openly suspicious of the offer, but he didn't say anything.

"After all," Truman explained, "y'all are like Sadie's family, and I guess we should find a way to get along."

Cal glanced suspiciously at the empty parking lot. "Is this a good place to eat?"

"I can honestly say that Sadie's Aunt Lillian is a great cook." *Six days out of the week.*

Together the five of them headed for the café. "So, what's cooking?" Mangino asked.

Truman smiled. "It's a surprise."

* * * * *

*The Benning Agency is about set
for another case!
Be sure to come back to
Intimate Moments for
ONE MAJOR DISTRACTION, IM 1372,
Linda Winstead Jones's next sexy, exciting
and surprising case....
Coming in June 2005!*

INTIMATE MOMENTS™

presents a provocative new miniseries by
award-winning author

INGRID WEAVER

PAYBACK

Three rebels were brought back from the brink and
recruited into the shadowy Payback Organization.
In return for this extraordinary second chance, they
must each repay one favor in the future. But if they
renege on their promise, everything that matters
will be ripped away...including love!

Available in March 2005:
The Angel and the Outlaw
(IM #1352)

Hayley Tavistock will do anything to avenge the
murder of her brother—including forming an
uneasy alliance with gruff ex-con Cooper Webb.
With the walls closing in around them, can love
defy the odds?

Watch for Book #2 in June 2005...
Loving the Lone Wolf
(IM #1370)

Available at your favorite retail outlet.

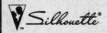

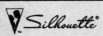

INTIMATE MOMENTS™

Don't miss the eerie
Intimate Moments debut
by

MARGARET CARTER

Embracing Darkness

Linnet Carroll's life was perfectly ordinary
and admittedly rather boring—until
she crossed paths with Max Tremayne.
The seductive and mysterious Max
claimed to be a 500-year-old vampire…
and Linnet believed him. Romance ignited
as they joined together to hunt down
the renegade vampire responsible for
the deaths of Max's brother and Linnet's
niece. But even if they succeeded, would
fate ever give this mismatched couple a
future together?

***Available March 2005
at your favorite retail outlet.***

COMING NEXT MONTH

#1351 SECOND-CHANCE HERO—Justine Davis
Redstone, Incorporated
Called to a crime-ridden tropical island, Redstone security chief
John Draven was reunited with Grace O'Conner, a single mother
recuperating from a devastating loss. Memories of what had happened
to this woman, what *he* had done to her, haunted him. When Grace's life
was put in jeopardy, would Draven be able to save her…again?

#1352 THE ANGEL AND THE OUTLAW—Ingrid Weaver
Payback
Grief-stricken Hayley Tavistock would do anything to avenge the
murder of her brother, a decorated cop. But she needed the help
of Cooper Webb, the hard-edged former thief who had his own
desperate reasons for pursuing this case with a vengeance. As sparks
and unanswered questions flew between them, Cooper and Hayley
were determined to find the killer before he struck again.…

#1353 HER SECRET AGENT MAN—Cindy Dees
Charlie Squad
To force banker Julia Ferrare into laundering money, her sister had been
taken hostage—by their father. Julia begged Charlie Squad, an elite Air
Force Special Forces team, for help. But she had a secret she needed to
hide from Dutch, the sinfully handsome agent sent to meet her. Once the
truth was revealed, would Dutch ever be able to forgive her?

#1354 STRANDED WITH A STRANGER—Frances Housden
International Affairs
Wealthy, pampered Chelsea Tedman never expected to be climbing
Mount Everest with a mysterious, alluring stranger. But only rugged
guide Kurt Jellic could get her up the cursed mountain to solve the
mystery of her sister's fatal fall. Would hidden dangers and passions
drive them into each other's arms…or plunge them to their own icy
demise?

#1355 EMBRACING DARKNESS—Margaret Carter
Until she met Max Tremayne, Linnet Carroll had led an ordinary
existence. But Max claimed to be a 500-year-old vampire…and
Linnet believed him. Now they needed to join together to hunt down the
renegade vampire responsible for the deaths of Max's brother and
Linnet's niece. Even if they succeeded, would this mismatched couple
ever be able to have a life together?

#1356 WORTH EVERY RISK—Dianna Love Snell
Branded with a wrongful conviction, Angel Farentino intended to prove
her innocence or die trying. As she ran for her life, she didn't need a
sexy savior distracting her. But undercover DEA agent Zane Jackson
had his own secrets—like discovering whether Angel was guilty of a
felony, or just guilty of stealing his heart. To find out, he needed to keep
her alive…a mission worth every risk.

SIMCNM0205